THE ASSASSINS

A SHATTERED ISLE NOVEL

JADE PRESLEY

ALSO BY JADE PRESLEY

The Shattered Isle series

Her Villains

Her Revenge

The Assassins

CONTENT WARNING

This book contains some depictions of emotional abuse, violence and gore, and sexual content with multiple consenting partners. I've taken every effort to handle these issues sensitively, but if any of these elements could be considered triggering to you, please take note.

If you've ever wanted the winter soldier to give you a hand necklace, this book is for you

1

GESSI

"I can't believe you agreed to this," Blaize snaps from behind me.

"She's our queen," River chides. "What would you have me do? Tell her no?"

"I would've," Varian chimes in, the hint of utter annoyance in his tone.

As usual, Crane is silent as the night where he brings up the rear of our little group.

I roll my eyes and whirl around on the rocks in which we're trekking over. "I am standing right exactly here," I say, looking at each of them and having a hard time disguising the intake of breath the sight inflicts upon me.

Truly, this group of males is one to marvel at. Each one is uniquely different and yet somehow just as annoyingly attractive. Varian and Crane I've known since we were younglings, but they've both grown into formidable males with skills and powers and muscles for nights on end.

But the two All Plane warriors? Stars damn me, I never thought it possible to be attracted to beings so inherently different. River is all sunshine and jokes and laughter with a body that's carved like a block of cedar, and Blaize? I don't even know how to describe him with his bedroom eyes, inky hair, and glittering silver tattoo along one arm that begs to be touched—the lines of artwork and stars traced.

Luckily for me, they're all insufferable and incessantly annoying with how seriously they take their duties as my personal guards—*thanks so very much, Cari.*

"Yes," Varian says, stepping up onto a craggy rock and towering over me. "We can see you, your highness. Just as well as we can see how ridiculous you look out here, braving the southern villages in some foolish attempt to lure out the general yourself." His tone is sharp, his eyes narrowed and this side of agitated.

"You should watch your tone with our queen," River says, arching a brow at Varian.

Varian points at him. "And I'd watch yours, pretty one," he says. "Lest I watch it for you."

River blows Varian a kiss, which only makes a growl rumble in his chest.

I blow out a breath, dismissing the two, and shift off the rock, heading for another one. They tried to stop me, tried to talk me out of venturing this far from the royal city, but it was no use.

"There have been attacks on this end of the Isle, attacks that scream of the general's penchant for torture," I say as I climb upon another rock, the sole of my flat shoes slipping slightly. "And I will *not* sit on my throne and wait for the monster to tear through what is left of my people. Like I said before, you all are with me or you're not." I spin around to face them, to show them how serious I am about not caring one way or another if they accompany me or not, but I lose my footing and fall backward, my spine no doubt aimed for the nearest, sharpest rock—

Strong, warm arms cradle me against an even harder chest. The scent of smoke and cedar swirl around me, sending a deep shiver right down the center of me as my eyes meet Blaize's. They're so light blue they're almost silver.

I swallow hard, my fingers digging into his leathers where he holds me against his chest—

"Clearly," Varian says, snapping me to attention. "You don't need our assistance, your highness."

Blaize blinks a few times before gently setting me on my feet and continuing ahead, clearly unaffected by me nearly plummeting to my death.

Maybe they're right. Maybe I'm in over my head. But am I really supposed to let that stop me from trying to spare my people any more hardship?

"If it's any consolation, my queen," River says as he walks by my side. "You fell utterly gracefully. Definitely no flailing of the arms or scrunched face." He presses his lips together, holding back a laugh that elicits one of my own.

I chuckle, shaking my head as we continue down the path. River, despite his antics with tinkering, always makes me laugh even when I don't want to. And I never knew how much I needed to laugh before he came into my life.

River winks, and my heart flutters as he walks ahead of me. It's an effort to *not* look at the three males ahead of me, their leathers clinging to every muscle and shift in their movements, but somehow, I manage it and forge ahead.

"Are you ever going to forgive me, Ges?" Crane's voice is a whisper at my back as he follows behind me.

I swallow around the lump in my throat, my heart clenching at all the things left unspoken between us these last weeks. He's tried on several occasions to explain his role in helping the general imprison me, but I've never let him. Yes, he helped me escape, but only after Cari showed up.

No, I can't hear his excuses, can't bear to hear how the mission was more important than me, than the friendship I'd thought we held.

I hold my head up high, searching for a response as we climb another bank of rocks along the path, the difficult terrain the only way to reach the southern villages on the Isle. The rocks are slick from the wind blowing the ocean all over them, and stars damn me, I slip again.

Crane's fingers are warm on my elbow as he steadies me, and lightning streaks through my veins at the innocent touch. I pause, my gaze locking on his. He shifts closer, his dark spice and rose scent spinning my senses.

"Maybe I should carry you, my queen," he whispers, something molten in his eyes as he trails them over the length of my body. "You seem to be having trouble staying on your feet today."

I swallow hard, heart racing. We're too close, the others too far ahead of us. My body wars with my heart, which he thoroughly broke when he tossed me in the cell at the general's command, when he stood guard at my door every single night and watched as they tortured me until I couldn't scream anymore.

Tears fill my eyes and I jerk out of his touch. "I'd rather fall and break my neck than let you touch me again," I snap, and Crane flinches.

I hurry ahead, reaching the others as we clear the last of the rocks, the mountainous terrain yawning open to the sandy beach hugging the obsidian ocean, and the village scattered about it.

"We're here," Varian says, but his voice is low, rough, and a muscle in his jaw ticks.

I follow his gaze and gasp at the sight of smoke curling from what is left of the village—huts and buildings burned and destroyed, ash floating on the breeze like fallen feathers from overhead birds.

I push past Varian and River, stumbling toward the wreckage, my heart cracking down the middle—

"Don't," Blaize says, his hand on my arm as he hauls me back.

"I have to help them," I say, tugging out of his embrace.

He hauls me back, wrapping his arms around me from behind, my back flush against his chest as he whisks us behind the nearest rock, shielding us from the sight of the ruined village. He spins me around to face him, his powerful hands on my shoulders, and his eyes locking on mine.

"Those fires are still burning," he whispers, his voice one hundred percent All Plane warrior. "Whoever did this is close. You can't be spotted."

"I can handle myself—"

"I know that," he snaps. "But you're the queen of the Shattered Isle. Your safety goes beyond your capabilities. What do you think happens to your Isle if you're taken prisoner or fall under an enemy blade?"

My chest rises and falls, panic climbing up my body at his words. He's right. Stars *damn* him, he's right.

"Do you have her?" Varian asks, no annoyance or cocky banter in his tone.

Blaize nods.

"We'll sweep it," he says, and motions to River and Crane, who follow him out of sight.

"Have me?" I glare up at him.

"I'll stop you," he says, shrugging. "If you try to run."

"I'm your queen—"

"And Steel asked me to protect you," he cuts me off. "That means I protect you, even from yourself." He presses closer, caging me between the rock and his body.

I tremble against him, some forbidden craving flaring to life inside me. Blaize is my personal guard and a near stranger. I have no business feeling...anything for him.

"Steel," I say, tilting my head. "Not your *king*?" I ask, referring to his best friend, one of Cari's mates who now also happens to be a king of the All Plane.

A slow, crooked smile shapes Blaize's lips. It's one of the first I've seen from him, and it makes my knees shake. "I'll never call Steel my king, and he knows it. An order from a king I can ignore," he says, and my brows raise at that. "But a favor for Steel?" he shakes his head. "I've never let him down before, and I don't intend to start now." He leans closer, eyes raking over every inch of my face. The breath in my lungs catches. "So, your highness," he says, and the title feels like a caress. "Are you going to make me stop you?"

My lips part. He's so close I can't breathe around his scent, can't feel the sea kissing my cheeks because his warm body is blocking it. There is nothing but his consuming presence, his power crackling between us—

"My queen," River calls from around the rock, and Blaize puts distance between us enough for me to breathe, enough for me to blink out of whatever haze he'd put me under. "It's clear," he says when he's rounded the rock, and extends his hand toward me. "But there is something you should see."

I spare one last glance at Blaize, unable to read the emotion in his light-blue eyes, before I take River's hand.

He keeps hold of mine as he guides me down the beach and amongst the wreckage until he stops before one home left completely intact.

I squeeze his hand in mine, drawing on his warmth and comfort to keep my knees from buckling. "Stars save us."

2

GESSI

The home is pristine. Not a lick of flame has touched it.

And I know why.

Splashes of color and artistry decorate one side of the home, the details taking my breath away.

It's a mural, an uncannily accurate illustration of myself, standing with a peaceful smile on my face, Cari—my best friend and now queen of the All Plane—by my side. Crowns of midnight and gold adorn each of our heads, and Cari's mates are standing behind her, the sun shining behind them. Behind me are my assassins, the stars twinkling in an inky sky behind them.

The Change We Need. Our Queens Will Provide is scrawled in delicate script at the bottom of the painting.

Whoever the artist is must've spent the last few weeks working on it.

It's gorgeous and heartwarming and hopeful.

Except for one thing.

Ice chills my blood as I drop River's hand and step closer to examine the still dripping red paint that is slashed over my and Cari's eyes. My stomach turns as I note the coloring, the consistency creating the giant X's over each of our eyes. It's not paint...

It's blood.

My fingers shake, rage bubbling as the smell of death and ash threatens to choke me.

"This is a fishing village," I say through my teeth, glaring at the blood on what was once a hopeful mural for these people. I glance toward the ever-churning ocean, balling my hands into fists. "One of our most successful ports. They were *peaceful*," I snap—not at my assassins—but at the burning village all around me.

The general. He did this. He set fire to an innocent village, simply because they supported me. Supported Cari.

Guilt and anger swirl together in a suffocating wave inside me. My powers thrash, desperate to slice into the general.

Wood snaps on either side of me, trees and branches bolting upward from the soft ground beneath my feet. Vines creak and twist around the wood, the sounds as angry as I feel—

A soft cough slices through my growing rage, the branches and vines disappearing as I rush toward the sound.

"Your highness!" River calls from behind me, but I ignore him as I race around the corner of the home.

I skid to a halt, instantly dropping to my knees beside the young female laying on her back, her hands clutching her stomach.

"My queen," she gasps, her voice weak. Her fingers are stained red, the once lavender color of her skin is leeched, drained. "You're here," she whispers as I reach for her. "I would bow, but I'm already on the ground beneath you."

She tries to laugh, but coughs up a mouthful of blood instead.

I clench her hand, barely moving it to see the gaping wound beneath.

"Help," I say, but it comes out a strained gasp as I look over my shoulder. "Help her."

My assassins surround me, River being the closest, all wearing somber looks. And I know they can't help her. *I* can't help her. We have no healers among us. No amount of our collective power can fix what's been done to her.

I turn back to her. "Who did this to you?"

She swallows hard. "There were twelve of them," she says. "They wore the uniform of Shattered Isle soldiers. We didn't think to question them...we thought you sent them. Then they started burning everything."

Tears gather behind my eyes, my body shaking with adrenaline. I grip her hand harder. "We'll get you help—"

"I'm beyond help," she says, and there is such peace on her face I can't help but tilt my head in confusion. "My mother was a healer. I've seen death all my life. The stars are close and the moon closer..." She coughs again, wincing as she looks beyond me to the night sky above. "I'm happy to die for something I believe in."

A tear rolls down my cheek and I lift my free hand, conjuring a shimmering night-blooming flower in my palm. I ensure the white petals glitter with silver dust on their tips, making it look like the moon and stars we love so much.

Her eyes light up as I place it on her chest.

"What is worth dying for?" I ask, swallowing around the lump in my throat.

She reaches with a bloodied hand and cups my cheek. "Peace. Hope. Everything you and Queen Cari stand for. You'll stop him. I know you will. I know—"

A rattled breath cuts through her words, her body stiffening before the light leaves her eyes. I hold her until River touches my shoulder, jerking me out of the ocean of emotions crashing inside me.

I blink and shift gently away from the female, directing my hand at the ground beneath her body. The earth yields to me. It always does. And I cover her body with soft, silky dirt and sprout night-blooming flowers over every place her blood spilled.

I blow out a shaky breath, turning to River. "Will you help me?"

"With anything," River immediately replies, stepping closer. "What do you need?"

Relief unravels some of the knots of rage inside me at his words, at the way his eyes are full of nothing but concern and support.

"We need to find the rest. They deserve to be buried too."

River nods, glancing at Varian, who falls into step without hesitation. Blaize heads the opposite direction, but Crane steps into my path when I move to follow him.

For a moment, I think he's going to fold me into his arms like he'd done so many times when we were younger.

Like the time some of the king's guards had stomped through my garden and destroyed it merely because they could. Crane had snuck into my quarters in the middle of the day to give me a rare seashell he must've spent the whole night searching for. He'd hugged me before he'd folded my hand around the shell, his silent comfort soothing the hurt.

I think now he might do the same, might press his cheek against mine and whisper words of encouragement and hope into my ear—

"You can't bury these people," he says.

Every thought and hope I had shatters.

I glare up at him. "Excuse me?"

His features shift to a plea. "It will only show whoever did this that you've been here. That you are not in the safety of your palace, but out here, in the open, exposed. Vulnerable to attack."

My lips part. "That's where your mind goes?" I jerk my arm toward the wreckage. "That female just died in my arms, and you're worried about our position being exposed?"

Crane visibly swallows as he moves closer. "I will *always* worry about your safety."

Pain lashes down the center of me. "Lies," I hiss. "You weren't worried when the general was carving me up night after night—"

"Ges," he cuts me off, anguish coloring his tone. "You have no idea. *None.* It would've been so much worse—"

"It couldn't have been any worse, Crane!" I cut him off.

Images of the general's blade digging into my flesh snaps across my vision. Or Erix—the general's right hand—and the claws he loved to use to carve up my skin.

The scars I bear from their torture prickle beneath my clothes.

"We bury them," I force the words out, ignoring the devastation on Crane's face. As if he cares about what happened to me, as if he's actually concerned about what *could* happen to me next.

Lies.

He would've stopped it if he cared. He would've sliced the necks of every guard who did the general's bidding while I was locked in that cell. Stars save me, *River*—who's only known me a matter of weeks—would have done it, had he been there. I know that with a certainty in my bones that makes little sense for two people who barely know each other. Or Varian. He would've shifted into his monstrous form and bit the heads off of every guard who touched me, he would've taken his time with the general had he known what was happening to me, but he hadn't even been on the Isle.

And Crane did nothing.

I shake my head, forcing the thoughts away.

"You bury these people and you might as well send a message to the general that you're here for the taking, that your *throne* is wide open for the taking—"

"We bury them!" I snap, my entire body shaking. The ground trembles beneath my feet as the earth responds to my rage. "These people died because they believed in me and Cari and our quest for peace between the realms. They died, defenseless and terrified. I will not leave their bodies for the crows when the sun comes up."

Crane parts his lips, as if he's about to argue again, but I hold up a hand, stopping him.

"Find the rest of them. Now. Or pick a grave site for yourself."

Crane flinches as I shove past him, following the path Blaize took moments ago.

And I don't dare look back.

3

RIVER

Dawn is just breaking over the horizon, painting the sky above the obsidian ocean in pinks and purples. My boots dig into the wet sand as I dip my dirty hands into the cool water, scrubbing my fingers and splashing a handful over my face.

"Never seen a pretty boy who was so good at getting his hands dirty," Varian says to my left as he shakes the water out of his chocolate brown hair. Drops of the ocean roll over the side of his face and down his neck, pooling on the black shirt that strains against his muscles.

He carries his strength around so casually—the muscles, the power radiating under his skin. I've caught a few glimpses of the beast that prowls beneath the surface, but he's never fully shifted in front of me yet. He hasn't needed to, thankfully, but Tor—my best friend and now one of the kings of the All Plane—told me enough about him when he assigned me to Gessi.

"I've always been good with my hands," I finally say, standing to face him.

He arches a brow at me, his features rippling with

mischief. His teal eyes trail the length of my body, slowly returning to my face.

We've adapted a casual banter since the second I stepped foot on the Shattered Isle, and normally, I'd love nothing more than to stand here and lobby back and forth with him...but today is different.

"I don't relish burying the dead with my hands though," I add a few moments later. "Not when they're innocent."

The playful teasing melts off of Varian's face, replaced with a severe look that only lasts a moment, but I catch it. I step closer to him, motioning the direction we just came from.

"Did you know them?" I ask.

Varian visibly swallows, then nods.

My gut sinks. We'd spent the entire night finding every lost innocent we could and burying whatever was left of their bodies from the wake of the flames. The fire hadn't claimed all of them, some were ended by a blade across their throats. Others had been tortured, evident in the way their faces were contorted in their last moments or the wounds decorating their bodies.

It had taken its toll on my queen, that much I could tell as we made our way back down the coast and made camp once we deemed it a far enough distance away from the carnage.

Varian focuses on the horizon, a muscle in his jaw working. "Gessi was right," he says, and I try not to flinch at the familiarity with which he addresses my new queen. They've known each other their whole lives and I get it—it's not like I can call Tor *my king* without laughing, but I can't help it... I'm *envious* of him. The way he knows her, the way she knows him. I want that. Have wanted it since the moment I laid eyes on her. On him, too.

"A fishing village," he continues. "Like Ges said. They supplied the palace and the royal city. They have for centuries. Never been violent or even disloyal, and they could've easily rebelled when Cari's father was on the throne." He shakes his head, his lips curling. "They didn't deserve this."

"I agree," I say, glancing over my shoulder toward where we made camp. Gessi's tent shivers slightly in the breeze, and I have the unshakable desire to go up there and wrap my arms around her, siphon off the guilt I know she's feeling. "Our queen blames herself."

Varian huffs out a dark laugh. "It's in her nature," he says, and I tilt my head. He shrugs. "Ges has always been like that. She's the first one to take the blame, take the responsibility. Carry the weight of anything that goes wrong. She's empathetic to a fault sometimes." He grins softly. "It was always worse on requesting night," he says. "Cari's father, the king, would allow people from all across the Isle to present requests to him and Cari one night a year. When Cari was old enough, he'd force her to hear all the needs, the complaints, the fears from the people. And Ges was always by her side, helping field all that built up hardship within the people brave enough to ask for help. By the end of it, both of them would be..." He hesitates, his eyes drawn and lost in the memory. "Not exhausted but...drained. As if they'd given all of themselves to those people, to try and help them with what little they could. Gessi especially. Crane and me would make sure to stay with them that week, playing card games or bringing them treats we'd stolen from the palace kitchens whenever we weren't training. Doing everything we could to help them shake off the stress of that event." He shakes his head. "Gessi still struggles with giving too much of herself, stretching herself too thin. The hardships, the things she can't fix...it eats away at her until some-times she doesn't have an ounce of energy or emotion left in her body and she has to be...reset."

"Reset?" I ask, wondering why he's talking about her like she's one of my gadgets that needs charging and rebooting on the regular.

He turns away from the ocean, tapping a finger against the center of my chest. "In here," he says. "Cari was the best at helping her find her way back to herself. Fill her up with love and laughter, all the things caring for those in need took from her." He glances over my shoulder. "Sometimes he'd do it." He nods toward Crane, who I can barely see perched atop one of the black, craggy coves that are scat-tered about the beach. "Other times it would be me." Some-thing flashes over his teal eyes, an emotion I can't read, but his full lips tilt up at the corners. "Guess you should learn that, pretty boy, seeing as you're one of us now."

I blow out a breath. "One of you?"

He claps me on the shoulder, his strong touch lingering a second. "A proper Shattered Isle assassin."

The title sends a jolt of lightning through my veins, or maybe it's the way he's looking at me. Maybe it's the idea of belonging to my new queen in such an official capacity, but either way, I don't hate it.

In fact, I thought I *would* hate it when Tor asked me to come and watch over Gessi. I didn't want to leave my home, my friends, everything I'd ever known to come to a place that's always been a cause of strain in my people's history. But I'd do anything for Tor, just like I know he'd do anything for me.

And *everything* changed the second I locked eyes with hers, all hazel and rimmed in black and full of hope. Some-thing shifted inside me, something I still can't explain. I only knew I would protect her at any cost and I lived for her soft smiles and optimistic hopes for the future.

Varian glances up to where Crane is still perched on the cove, and without another word, heads off in that direction.

I stand for a moment, listening to the waves crash behind me. There is no sign of Blaize. If he wants to be found, he will. So, I do the only thing my instincts will allow —I make the trek toward my queen's tent and pause outside of the closed flap of silk rustling in the wind.

Everything inside me is stretching out like a rope tethered to an anchor.

"You can come in, River," Gessi calls through the closed fabric, jarring me slightly.

I pull back the silk, closing it after I duck inside.

Someone—I'm guessing Crane—set this up for her, because the ground is cushioned with the piles of blankets we'd carried in our packs. She sits in the middle, her gorgeous jade skin clean of the dirt she'd been covered in earlier, a fresh soft shirt and loose shorts covering her. The smell of orchids and the ocean fills her small tent, and I immediately relax at the sight of her.

"How did you know it was me?" I ask, standing at the edge of her tent, awkwardly hunched over from how tall I am and how small the tent is. Really, it's only big enough for five people, and even then, it would be pushing it. Sure, I could activate my suit and shrink my size, but I really only like to do that in battle or when playing a prank on Tor.

"Deduction," she says, her eyes drawn downward as she runs her hand back and forth over the blanket. "Crane is furious with me and left once he set up my tent, even though I assured him I could do it myself. Blaize spared me a glance before disappearing farther down the coastline, and Varian..." She shakes her head, finally looking up at me.

I'm almost brought to my knees by how stunning her hazel eyes are, how beautiful she looks, even with sadness and exhaustion shaping her features.

"Varian wouldn't have been polite enough to hesitate. He would've barged in if he needed something," she finishes.

My shoulders sink at her logic and I mentally kick myself for the disappointment. Did I really expect her to feel the same way I do? After only a few weeks? Even *I* know it's ridiculous to feel this connection to her in such short a time, but I can't ignore it.

"Clever queen," I say.

She furrows her brow at me. "You can sit, you know," she says, motioning to the small space across from her. "You don't have to stand all hunched over like that."

"I didn't want to intrude…"

"You're not," she assures me. "I don't really want to be alone right now." I move to sit, but her eyes go wide and apologetic. "Not that I'm ordering you to sit! It's not an order, just a request…" She clenches her eyes shut, and I laugh at the way she's flustered.

I take a seat across from her, balancing my forearms on my knees as a genuine smile shapes my lips.

"Don't laugh," she says, eying me, but there is a lightness in her tone that wasn't there moments ago. "I'm horrible at this queen stuff." The severity of her words catches up to her and her head dips. "Cari made a mistake," she whispers, and it takes me a second to work out what she means.

"Don't say that—"

"She did," she cuts over me. Her delicate fingers graze the necklace around her throat, the one Talon made for her to stay connected to Cari. CB-2—I believe that's what Cari called it. "She should've chosen someone else. Someone raised to be a queen—"

"You may not have any formal training," I say. "But that doesn't mean you weren't *born* to be a queen." Her breath catches as I boldly reach over and tilt her chin up to meet my eyes. "Cari was raised as an assassin, and she's already one hell of an All Plane queen. Trust her judgment. You are going to change the realms."

"But this village, these people, they died because they supported me. Supported Cari."

"They died because a sadistic dictator ordered them to be burned and bloodied. They died for no other reason."

"If they didn't openly support me, they wouldn't have died!" she snaps. "They could've bent the knee to the general's demands and *lived*."

"That's not living," I say.

She parts her lips to argue, but then closes them, acceptance fluttering over her features.

Silence fills the space between us and I swear I can *feel* her hopelessness and guilt as if it were my own. "You know this is just the beginning, right?"

Shock widens her eyes.

"I'll never lie to you, my queen," I hurry to say. "The last thing I want to do is hurt you, but you have to be prepared for what's coming. I don't want you to put yourself in harm's way because of the guilt."

She tilts her head. "You act like you know me," she says, a light tease in her voice.

"I feel like I know you better than I should, given our short time together, but tell me I'm wrong. Tell me you won't sacrifice yourself if that's what it takes to stop the general."

She stays quiet, and the answer in the silence sends a wave of panic crashing over me. The idea of her doing such a thing makes me feel like I've just stepped off the edge of a cliff.

"Good thing my deadly assassins also offer wise council," she says, and some of the tension eases from my chest. "Well, some of them." Pain flickers in her gaze, and I want to break Crane's nose. I know that's who she's referring to because Varian and her are friendly, and Blaize and I are too new to have wounded her so deeply.

She rubs her temples, and my fingers itch to do the job for her. And not stop at just that innocent touch. I crave so much more from her. I want to know if her skin is as soft as it looks, want to know the taste of her on my lips, and the feel of her body against mine.

I clear my throat, shoving down the insatiable desire for someone I barely know, not to mention my *queen*. My duty is to protect her, serve her, not fantasize about her.

"Have you eaten?" I ask.

She shakes her head, and I immediately get up, grabbing my pack I left outside the tent. I return, already digging out some bread and fruit and cheese we packed for the trip. I hand her my canteen first, and she takes a sip.

"Is it awful of me to wish this was wine?" she asks.

I grin at her as I fix up a cloth full of food. "Not at all," I say, handing it to her.

"Thank you," she says, nibbling on a berry.

I take a few bites of my food and we eat in a comfortable silence for a while.

"You've been around death before, haven't you?" she asks, and I raise my brows. "I don't mean that in a bad way," she hurries to add. "I just mean...you handled yourself around the carnage well today."

"I've been in a few battles." More like too many to count over my some two-hundred years. "Thanks to Tor's appetite for brawls and the All Plane's affinity to draw attacks, I've seen more than my fair share."

"You and Tor have been best friends for a long time?"

I nod. "Since we were younglings. Like you and Cari, from what I've heard."

A small smile shapes her lips, and it lights up my heart. "Do you regret him sending you to me? I'm sure you miss him. I know I miss Cari."

"I miss him. I miss the way the sun glides over the palace like warm honey, but there is something to be said about the night, about the stars and the way they shine here like they do nowhere else."

"Isn't that kind of talk frowned upon where you come from?"

"It used to be, yes. The previous king would've seen fit to throw me in a dungeon and beat the star admiration out of me. But Cari has changed that. You're both going to change everything. For the better."

She sits up a little straighter, almost like my words are filling her up, like much-needed air in her lungs. Varian's words from earlier make more sense now, and I resign myself to making sure I pay close attention to whenever Gessi gives too much of herself away.

Like today.

She gave and gave and gave. I know she pushed her powers to the dregs and is probably suffering for it now.

"I can't believe you don't resent me," she says, shaking her head. "For being ordered to my side—"

"Tor didn't order me," I cut her off. "He asked me and I agreed."

"And you have no regrets?"

"Not one," I say, then tilt my head. "Except..." I hesitate. I said I'd never lie to her, and I meant it, but that doesn't mean I need to expose myself so quickly.

"Except?" she asks, leaning forward, her food finished,

the cloth discarded to the side. She's so close as she hangs in the moment, so close I could sweep her into my lap in one simple move.

I tilt toward her too, never breaking her gaze, desperate to get closer, to touch her, taste her.

"Except what, River?" she whispers, almost a plea. We're inches apart now, her sweet floral scent washing over me, making my head spin. I bet she tastes sweet too.

"Except," I say, looking from her lips to her eyes and back again. "I regret I didn't meet you sooner." There. The truth of what I've felt since I walked onto this isle.

Her eyes flutter, a small breath leaving her lips. She hesitates, the moment stretching tight between us. I can't move. I'm grounded in this, forcing myself to stay still when all I want to do is haul her against me. But this is my queen and I will never go where I'm not wanted.

"River," she says, and I nearly groan at the sound of my name on her lips like that, all breathless and needy.

"Yes, my queen?" I ask, holding her gaze.

She inches closer, her lips only a breath away.

Dangerous.

This is testing every limit I've ever set on myself and giving in and fucking my queen would definitely be a limit I'm not meant to break. I'm sure there is a rule somewhere. Right?

"I need..." She hesitates, lingering just on the edge of touching me, and my willpower is about to snap. My cock is already straining in my leathers, begging to sink into her, to claim her, to worship her until the pain she's experienced today is erased and replaced with nothing but pleasure.

"Tell me what you need," I say, my entire body buzzing. Fuck, I should get out of here. I should run out of this tent right this second and dive into the icy ocean. I should stop this. I'm her assassin and protector, nothing more. I can't be more.

Her eyes are hooded, glazed with something I can't ignore, and fuck it, I'm about to disregard every royal politeness and duty I've ever been taught.

"I need—"

"We need to talk about our next steps," Varian says as he barges into the tent, just like Gessi said he would.

Gessi and I dart away from each other, enough that Varian looks up from the map he'd been focused on, and wags a finger between the two of us, a smirk playing over his full lips.

"Wait a second," he says, drawing out his words. "Did I just interrupt something interesting?" He cocks a brow at Gessi, not even bothering to hide the lust in his eyes.

Then he glances at me and the heat in his look only makes my cock twitch again. I can't help it. He's pretty damn hard to ignore and I've never stayed in one lane when it came to sex—and back home I'd been lucky to have several formidable, casual partners—but here? I've only wanted Gessi, the one female I can't have, and Varian? Well, from the way he's looking at us both, he wouldn't mind joining in on what may or may not have happened had he not barged in.

Blaize follows in behind him, scanning the small space in the cold, calculating way he does, before folding his arms over his chest.

Crane is the last to enter, the three males crammed in and hunched over in the tiny tent. Suddenly it's hard to breathe. There is way too much power swirling around the small space.

Gessi must feel it too, because she shifts on the blanket,

as if she needs to either get closer or back away. I'm not sure which.

"We only have enough time for a couple hours rest," Crane says before glaring at me.

I'm tempted to toss him a vulgar gesture, but I stay quiet by my queen's side.

"Then we need to make our way back to the palace," he says.

"What? No. We need to warn the neighboring villages of the potential danger," Gessi argues.

"You can assign someone to do that," Crane says. "You're needed back at the palace."

She narrows her gaze at him. "Last time I checked, Crane," she says, her voice filled with venom, "you are not the queen of the Shattered Isle—"

"You're right," he says. "I'm not. You are. And you can't rule a realm from the coast. You're needed at home."

"My people need to know that I care."

"They will. Send one of us for all I care. Just go home, Ges."

She flinches at the delicate plea in his voice, at the tender way he says her name. Even I feel sorry for him at that moment. Then I remember he left her to be tortured by the general and his men and want to murder him all over again.

"He has a point, love," Varian says, his eyes all sorts of soft and pleading as he looks at her. He can really put it on when he wants to. Prick. "We can warn the villages. Help them make preparations if need be. Your people need you to rule."

"Fine," she snaps, glaring at Crane. "You go. Warn as many as you can." She looks to Varian, Blaize, and then me. "You three are with me."

Crane's hard jaw looks like it's about to break, he's clenching it so hard, but he nods once, and disappears out of the tent.

"Ouch," Varian says, shaking his head. "I hope whenever you two sort out your shit you'll invite me, because it's going to be explosive."

"That's all, Varian," Gessi says, waving a hand to him and Blaize. "I need to sleep if we're going all the way back home."

Blaize nods and heads out of the tent, but Varian lingers.

"Is that an invitation, love?" he teases, and I can't help but laugh at the look on his face. He's goading her and he knows it.

"In your dreams, Varian," she says, a fire in her eyes that replaces the hurt from when Crane was here seconds ago. I admire Varian just a little more for what he's doing. Distracting her, teasing her, getting her mind anywhere else than on the male she just dismissed like yesterday's garbage.

He leans over, just enough to get in her space, and lowers his voice. "Oh, I *do* dream about it, Ges. Frequently."

Suddenly, I feel like I'm intruding on an intimate moment, but with him blocking the way out, it's not like I can sneak out unnoticed.

"Do you?" he asks when she seems frozen to the spot. Her chest rises and falls, the pulse in her neck thumping rapidly.

Oh, now I'm really intrigued. Do they have more than a friendly history?

Varian holds her gaze for a few more moments, then winks at her before spinning out of the tent. "Anytime, Ges," he calls from outside the tent. "You know that."

She blows out a breath, shaking her head.

I want to ask her what it means, but I know it's not my

place. Instead, I get up, dipping my head to her as I linger at the tent's opening. "Get some rest, my queen," I say. "I'll wake you when it's time to go."

"River," she says as I turn. I pause and glance over my shoulder. There is something there, on her face, a lingering need or unanswered question, but she says nothing else. She merely smiles at me, then lays down with her back to me.

The ache in my chest intensifies the farther I walk away from her tent, the farther I get from her, and I'm left wondering what might've happened if Varian hadn't barged in.

And whether or not I'm happy that he did.

4

CRANE

"Come on. Scream for me." The general's guard—Erix —sinks a meaty fist into Gessi's left side, and I swear I can feel the impact as if he hit me.

Gessi doesn't scream.

She never screams anymore.

She's strung up by those horrible power-nullifying chains in her cell, and Erix is torturing her while the general watches from the corner.

"I will break you," the guard says, throwing another punch.

A whimper escapes her lips, but she keeps her jaw tight, her eyes defiant as she sucks in a sharp breath.

Three nights of this already. My soul is shredded, ripped, flayed.

I can't stop it. If I did...it would be so much worse for her.

She hates me, but I'd rather endure her hatred than see her ruined.

The general pushes off the wall from where he lingers, stopping in front of Ges. I can see him as clearly as if I were in the room. I've always been able to see, even if there is only a small sliver of space to spy through.

My gift and my curse.

Because I don't want to see this.

Don't want to see the general's razor-sharp teeth as he sadistically grins at Gessi.

Don't want to see the blade he pulls from a sheath on his wrist.

Don't want to see her hunter green blood spill in drops on the floor, all while she does her best not to scream.

But I see it all.

And I want to die.

I bolt upright in bed, a knife in my hand and sweat beading on my brow. I scan my room, my mind taking a few seconds to remember where I am.

Home. I'm home. Not in the dungeons. Not outside what used to be Gessi's cell.

I slide the knife back in its place under my pillow and rake my hands over my face as I catch my breath.

The room is still slightly unfamiliar to me with its lush carpets, elaborate tapestries, and feather bed. I've only slept in here a few weeks, moved in right after Gessi was named queen and me one of her elite assassins. I wanted to be closer to her, even though she hates me more than the general himself. And she has every reason to. She thinks I betrayed her.

I've tried telling her the truth, but she won't listen to me.

At least she's alive, *whole*.

I swing my feet over the bed and stretch as I walk toward my window. It has a little balcony that overlooks the ocean far below. The sun sets slowly over the horizon as I slip onto the balcony, settling into a comfortable position as I scan the empty, quiet beach.

Gessi selected this room for me, almost as if she knew I'd prefer this view over the other rooms on the opposite side of the palace that overlook the royal city. Hope flickers to life in my chest that maybe, just maybe, there is still something there between us. Some modicum of feeling for me, to choose a room that suits me so well.

Who am I kidding? She'll never forgive me. Never understand.

I watch the sun set in a weighted silence, thinking of the fishing village from two weeks ago, thinking of the other coastal villages I warned while Gessi and Varian and River and Blaize made the trek back here. I only just returned yesterday and I haven't seen her. I *ache* to set eyes on her, to know she's safe.

The general is ruthless—he trained me to be ruthless, to kill without regret, without hesitation. Unlike Cari—who had to be not only ruthless but loveable to the public—I was never trained to be anything other than the perfect assassin. One you never see coming.

The things he'll do to her now that she sits on the throne he's lusted after for centuries.

Ice stings my blood, urging me to move. I dress in my fighting leathers, sling my bow over my back and breathe a little easier as the familiar, comforting weight settles between my shoulders.

Night has awoken and so has the palace. The staff is stirring, preparing for the night, and Gessi...she'll be making her way to the breakfast hall to eat before she has to see to the people's requests.

It's selfish of me to seek her out. She'd be better off hating me and never setting eyes on me again, but I can't leave her. Even the two weeks I was gone, warning the villages, I wanted her, dreamed about her, reached for her even though she was miles away. It's always been that way between us. Since we were younglings, always reaching for the other and never truly connecting.

Because how could I let such a beautiful, hopeful, *good* female like herself be marred by the darkness of what I'd been raised to be? The general selected me, selected Varian, and twisted us until we didn't recognize the younglings we used to be. Creatures who most certainly aren't worthy of a queen like Gessi, not that that would ever stop Varian.

Or River, apparently.

I freeze in the entryway of the breakfast hall. River is smiling and laughing on Gessi's right side. The All Plane bastard has her eyes lighting up as she sips her juice, making her laugh so hard she nearly spits out the drink.

I don't see the nobility of the Shattered Isle filling the tables below the queen's on the raised dais. I don't hear them gossiping or chatting. I only see Gessi, hear her laugh.

Jealousy twists and writhes in my gut. Not that I'm not up for sharing, but because *he* is making her smile. A genuine smile shapes her lips, the one she used to give to me before everything happened. I cherished those moments, savored them like a much-needed meal.

She doesn't smile at me like that anymore.

She never will.

And I hate River on principle.

I swallow down the acidic taste in my mouth, lift my chin, and enter the room. My boots are silent against the tiled floor as I move swiftly across the room, loading up my plate at the food station and taking my assigned seat at the queen's table.

Gessi's laughter dies the second I sit two spots down from her, just on the other side of Blaize. Varian sits on the other side of River, tearing into his meat and eggs like a wild dog.

"You're back," Gessi almost whispers the words, and I give her a curt nod. She swallows hard, her eyes flickering with pain and regret and something else I can't figure out. In a blink, it's replaced with a cold, hard look. "Did you run into any trouble?" she asks, her voice strong and clear, a true queen's voice.

Good, maybe she's finally adjusting to her new role. Maybe these two weeks at the palace have helped her settle into the crown that sits atop her head—all silver with black diamonds and engraved with stars.

"No," I answer, my voice softening simply because I'm speaking to her. It's an effort, since our last few conversations have been short, painful, and sharp.

"Good," she says, looking at me as if she's waiting for me to elaborate.

"I warned every village on the southern coast. They've made preparations, but I saw no sign of the general or his guards. Those I spoke with hadn't heard or seen anything of them either."

She nods and holds my gaze, almost as if she's hoping I'll say more, hoping I'll keep talking.

But what else can I say? Especially with her new favorite male by her side? And Blaize and Varian, have they too moved up her favorites list? A top spot I used to hold before...before...

Before I let her down.

Before the general threatened to ruin her.

But he couldn't ruin her, not with me doing as he ordered. And now here she sits, a crown atop her head and laughter in her heart. I'll gladly pay the price for that every night for the rest of my life.

Something like broken glass scrapes my insides as I see her bottom lip quiver at my lack of offering her something more, and I part my lips, desperate to take the pain away, but she shakes her head as she pushes away from the table.

"I'll be in the throne room," she says, eyes landing on River.

"I'd love to accompany you, my queen," he answers her unspoken question, and I roll my eyes, my fists clenching around the fork and knife in my hands. They've already reached silent communication? Are they fucking too?

That's not fair. Gessi is free and able to choose as many lovers as she wants.

Still, I fucking hate him for it.

"You're not bored?" Gessi asks, her voice all silk and softness. "This will be your fourth time this week."

River rises from the table, and I hate the way his custom red leathers make him look...*regal*. Like he belongs next to my friend, wearing her crown like she was born for it. And she was, she really was.

"Nothing is ever boring where you're involved," he says, grinning down at her. The look they share makes my stomach turn. There is something there, something intense and beautiful, if I'm being honest.

She deserves that and more.

But I still picture shooting an arrow through one of his pretty green eyes.

I set down the fork, watching as they walk out of the room together, comfortable and easy around each other, even in their movements.

My fingers twitch toward my bow. One shot. That's all it would take—

"You do that and she'll spend an entire month peeling back your skin with nothing but those spikey branches she loves to create," Varian says, not bothering to look up from where he's buttering his toast.

I glare at him. He always knows. We were trained as assassins together, graduated to the elite class together. We can sense the other, anticipate each other's moves before we make them. Incredibly handy during a battle, terribly annoying when you're contemplating killing the newest member to join your little team.

I part my lips, but Varian points his butter knife at me. "Don't even think about denying it," he says, finally looking at me. "Pretty boy is the queen's favorite," he continues, taking a massive bite of his toast. "I'd hate to have to kill *you* for killing her favorite."

A smirk shapes my lips, the first bit of lightness I've felt in weeks. Give it to my best friend to be the one to offer it to me. "Now who's lying?" I ask, returning to my breakfast. "You've been dying for a shot at killing me ever since that drunken night I beat you at cards. You picked a fight with me and I put you on your ass."

Blaize leans forward in his chair, the silent, cold warrior's eyes flickering with intrigue. "Go on," he says, which has both me and Varian turning toward him, since he rarely says anything. "I'd love to hear how you bested Varian."

Varian laughs, shaking his head. "Even he doesn't believe it, Crane," he says. "If I hadn't been drunk, you never would've stood a chance."

I scoot back from my chair, rising to the challenge. I move quicker than he can follow, my fist drawn back—

A black, tentacle like muscle blocks me, almost swallowing my fist whole as it drags me closer to where Varian sits. He's still eating his toast with one hand, but the other he's shifted into his creature form, holding my fist captive.

I flick out a blade with my free hand and press the tip to

the mass around my trapped fist. "I'll cut it off, Varian, I swear to the stars!"

Varian laughs, drawing me closer still as he drops his toast and stands up. We're nearly chest to chest now, adrenaline surging through my blood at the prospect of a good fight. After everything, I could really fucking use one.

"No, you won't," Varian says, a challenging look on his face. "You know I'd break every bone in your hand first, and I know how much you *love* this hand." He squeezes my fist tighter, the sensation painful and pleasant at the same time. I dig the blade in just enough for him to feel the kiss of its edge—

Blaize stands up, stomping over to stand beside the two of us. "Everyone is looking," he whispers.

Varian and I glance out at the breakfast hall, noting the other Shattered Isle guards, the staff, and nobility have paused eating their breakfast and are focused on us. No doubt one of them is about to run off and tell the queen about her assassins bickering like younglings.

"Soldier boy is right," Varian says, unraveling his creature arm from me.

"Don't call me that," Blaize says through clenched teeth as I shake out my fist.

"What?" Varian shrugs. "You're an All Plane soldier, are you not?"

Blaize rolls his eyes, the muscles in his arms flexing, the one covered in silver tattoos—with one lone red star disrupting the silver—bulging more than the rest. I've yet to find out exactly what powers he possesses, but I can feel the rise between the three of us, the powers clashing against each other, and I know his is almost as strong as Varian's.

Varian sits back down, returning to his breakfast as if nothing happened. "Any time either of you want to be humbled, I'm more than happy to handle that in the training ring."

I huff out a laugh, returning to my breakfast.

Blaize, having cleaned his plate, disappears from the room, leaving nothing but a cold curiosity in his wake.

And by the time Varian and I finish, I'm left with more tension than when I entered the room. Because now that I'm back, now that I'm officially Gessi's assassin again, I have no idea how to be what she needs versus what will protect her in the end.

5

GESSI

I've been the Shattered Isle queen for almost six weeks now and somehow, I still feel like a youngling playing pretend. Although, whenever Cari and I *did* play pretend, we never chose to be queens. We'd choose to be chefs or gardeners or sailors—things that were so forbidden to us they seemed fantastical. Crane and Varian would indulge us, conjuring up their own characters to play off of ours.

Ages ago. Eons ago. Even under the hardships Cari faced, it seemed easier than now.

"We've stretched our efforts along the edges of Sand's Swallow," Lance, the newest appointed leader of the Shattered Isle assassins, says.

He oversees training of the new recruits, plus carries out my orders with his seasoned assassins. Crane recommended him for his loyalty to Cari and now to me, back when we were dispatching disloyal Shattered Isle assassins left and right.

I refused to continue the elite assassin training—the same training Varian and Crane were subjected to. It was one of my first decrees as queen. No male or female will ever be forced into that kind of brutality again.

"And?" I ask when Lance looks less than keen to continue.

"There have been no signs or whispers of the general's whereabouts."

My heart sinks and I grip the edges of my chair in the council room a bit more tightly. River sits on my right, stoic and supportive. Blaize is in the farthest corner of the room, silently scanning and assessing everything with those wintry blue eyes of his. Crane is likely perched on one of the balconies above the room, not that I care to notice, and Varian sits on my left, flipping a blade end over end, his face the picture of boredom.

"Double your efforts," I finally say, and Lance immediately dips his head. "But ensure that your assassins are properly fed and have the supplies they need. Whatever you need, we'll make it happen. I don't want the search weakening you or your team." Because we may very well need their strength should the general ever show his face.

Where in the stars is he?

"Pretty, pretty flower," the general says as he rakes a blade over my ribs. The sting rips a whimper from my lips, one I kick myself for. I don't want to give him the satisfaction of my pain. "Bleeds pretty as its petals," he continues, working that knife over my skin. "Tell me how your precious princess keeps finding out where my assassins are going, and I'll let you lick your wounds in peace."

My eyes meet his, tears rolling down my cheeks. Traitorous tears I can't stop. The pain burns and sears and aches. There is so much of it. Too much of it. But I can't...I'll never give him what he wants. If these chains weren't wrapped around my wrists, I'd send a poisonous barbed branch right through his eye and be done with it.

He knows my power, knows what I can do with it. And he's never played fair, neither does King Jerrick. That's why they searched the entire Shattered Isle for these horrible chains, searched for the rare stone that nullifies powers, stripping you down to the weakest version of yourself.

I glance toward the door, at the little slat in the wood. Hopeful, desperate. Crane has to be out there. Varian is off the Isle. He doesn't know where I am, but Crane. He's here. I know he is—

"Who are you looking for?" The general grips my chin, jerking my face back to his. His nails are filed to points, biting into my flesh. "No one is coming to save you. You think you're worth defying my orders? Little flower, you have no idea how good I've been to you. I can do worse. I will do worse if you don't talk."

My body shakes, fear snapping its teeth along my body. I can feel the malicious intent in the general's power like an oil slicking over my skin.

I know what he's done is only the beginning.

But I'll never betray Cari.

I tip my chin, willing my body to stop shaking.

The general grins, his pointed teeth gleaming like a sea creature approaching its dinner. He takes a step away, motioning to one of his lackeys.

I stop breathing. Erix.

Not him. He's the most vicious of my torturers, save for the general.

He smiles as he stands before me, taking the general's place. Claws protrude from his fingers, his face only partially shifting into the cat-like creature that prowls beneath his skin.

I brace myself, closing my eyes as I search for a better place, any place, to retreat.

Anywhere but here.

The spring meadows from my home, the little cottage in the Earth Realm I can barely remember. The smell of fresh-cut grass and flowers and—

Sharp pain bites into my right side, and my eyes snap open as my body jerks against the assault. Erix's claws are dug into my side, shredding my flesh like I'm made of silk. Warmth trickles down my side, my blood slicking my skin, my eyes blurring at the edges as he digs those claws in deeper. I hiss against the pain, and glare at him as he smiles, as he gets off on this. I thrash in my chains, desperate to unleash my powers. Stars know where his claws have been. I'll likely die from some heinous infection the nasty brute picked up somewhere.

The ridiculous thought makes me laugh. A dark, delusional laugh that wipes the smile clean off Erix's face. Because how can I worry about a death like that, when the general is intent on keeping me alive long enough to slowly peel me apart?

"Laugh, little flower," the general says from behind Erix. "Laugh all you want. It'll only make this that much more fun."

Erix claws at my chest, leaving lines of hunter green down the center, and my laughter dies.

And after the next slash, I don't remember what was funny.

"Your highness?" Lance's voice cuts through my memory, and River's hand is over mine, which still clenches the wooden armrest of my chair. River is looking at me with concern all over his features, and it hits me straight in the chest.

Stars, I'm tired.

Tired of feeling like glass.

Tired of feeling like the memories that haunt me will break me at any moment.

Tired of feeling like a fraud in a crown.

"Yes?" I ask, glancing from River to Lance apologetically.

"Is there anything else you need from me?" he asks, as if he's already asked it.

"That will be all, Lance," I say. "Thank you again for your efforts."

Surprise flickers across his features, just like it's done every time I've thanked him for his hard work. The Shattered Isle assassins aren't used to thanks and I honestly don't know if they ever will be, but it feels wrong *not* to thank him. He's loyal and respectful and has made every effort to do my bidding. I don't understand a king or queen who wouldn't be grateful to those who support them.

Lance dips his head, then leaves the council room, his six top guards following behind him. I blow out a breath, sinking farther back in my chair.

"You need me to stab something, love?" Varian asks, still flipping that knife end over end. He flashes me that mischievous smirk of his that I've always been a sucker for, then winks.

And a laugh tumbles from my lips, breaking the chains weighing me down.

River draws his hand away from mine, the tension easing in his shoulders too.

"Not unless you can stab a nightmare," I say, sighing.

Varian leans over the table, his leg brushing mine beneath it. Sparks erupt beneath my skin, my body remembering...*other* memories. Happier, wild memories that cause an ache to wrench low in my core.

"You'd be surprised what all I'm capable of stabbing," he says, his teal eyes bright.

I laugh again. "Actually, I don't think I would be surprised."

River laughs then, and the memory of the general's and Erix's torture drifts away.

I pinch the bridge of my nose as Blaize makes his way to the table, taking a seat now that the room is clear of everyone but us.

"What do you need?" Blaize asks, and the sincerity in the question steals my breath. Blaize is a male of few words, but when he's near, there is an intensity between us I can't deny. Somehow, I know he'd do anything for me and for some irrational reason, I feel I would do anything for him.

It's the same for River, and Varian, of course, but it's been that way between us for a very long time. I can't deny the sensations for my newest companions or rationalize it, but I've stopped trying. I'm exhausted down to my bones— trying to be the queen my isle needs right alongside the huntress I need to be to capture the general. Once again, I feel the urge to take my four assassins and hunt for him myself. It's as overwhelming as it is ridiculous, because as much as I hate to admit it, Crane is right about me needing to protect the throne during such a vulnerable transition.

"I need..." I take a deep breath, exploring the question down to the roots of my being as I look at the three assassins, eyes on me, prepared and willing to give me whatever I ask for. Something hot and needy curls inside me, reaching out to each of them on instinct, and I swear I see the three of them tense at the same time.

But that doesn't make sense.

None of this makes sense. Not the position I'm in, the queendom I'm now ruling, or the needs I feel when my assassins are in the same room as me.

I want them.

All of them.

Even the onlooker from the balcony, the one I don't have to *see* to know he's there. I feel him, just as strongly as I can now feel River and Blaize and Varian. Maybe it's just the connection of their assigned roles to me. Maybe it's because they've been with me through this heavy transition. Either way, I can't stop the need from rising, twisting, and coiling so much it aches.

"You need a drink," Varian finishes for me, and I laugh again.

"Yeah," I breathe out the word. "I really think I do. Don't all of you?"

"I could use one," Blaize admits and River nods.

"Is that allowed?" I ask, eyes darting between the three of them. "With everything going on? Shouldn't I be...I don't know, planning more?"

"You can't find the general with willpower alone," River says. "If you could, he'd already be dead."

That's the truth.

"And you've done everything in your power to protect the Isle from whatever he's planning," River continues. "You have every available assassin scouring the Isle for him as we speak. You can't ask more of yourself than that."

"Besides," Varian says, pushing back from the table. "You're the Shattered Isle queen. You can do whatever the fuck you want."

Blaize is the next to rise, looking at Varian. "Where are we headed?"

Varian smirks. "I know just the place."

I FLOP BACK DOWN on one of the oversized cushions that cover the floor in Varian's favorite parlor room—one of twelve in the palace. Varian brought us here a few hours ago.

"All right, no more wine for the queen," Varian teases, and I roll my eyes as I reach for my still half-full glass.

"I've only had *one*," I say, sipping the slightly sweet white wine that sparkles in my glass.

"Says the queen who just nearly *fell* on her face," Varian says, downing his third glass.

"You told me to show you my defensive stance!"

"I didn't think you'd do it!"

River laughs where he lounges to my right, and I arch a brow at him. "Don't you start thinking he's funny too," I playfully chide him.

"I can't help it, my queen," he says, motioning his glass toward Varian. "It's hard not to."

Varian blows a kiss our direction. "I'm irresistible in every way, love. You of all people should know that," he says, and warmth unfurls in my core.

Memories of his lips on my skin erupt in a rapid flash behind my eyes. Stars, how long ago was that night? What would he do if he knew I haven't let another male touch me since? I can almost feel the graze of his teeth on my neck...

I have to shift on the cushion to relieve some of the tension.

Blaize's blue eyes are on me from where he sits across from me, languid and relaxed for once, and I swear he sees right through me. That All Plane warrior misses nothing.

Crane remains in the corner of the room, silent as a statue, his glass of wine untouched. I don't know why he bothered to join us in our rare night of relaxation if he's content to brood all night. After a few sips of wine, my anxiety has eased as I allow myself to escape the pressures of the last few weeks for just a night, and I'd even go as far as to at least chat with him if he initiated it.

Which he hasn't.

Blaize and Varian and River, on the other hand, have kept me so entertained these past few hours that I can't stop smiling. My sides hurt from laughing so much and it's been more than refreshing to see Blaize loosen up, telling stories about Steel and what they would get up to when they were younglings. Slowly, I can see the bond between all of us growing stronger, which is a relief since we were all thrown into new roles during a dangerous time for both our realms.

No, nope. Not going there. Not thinking about it. Tomorrow there will be time to be Queen Gessi with the weight of the realms on her shoulders, but tonight...tonight I just want to be...*theirs*.

My assassins.

My friends.

The males who've meant more to me these past weeks than I can truly express. Without Cari by my side, they've filled the role of friendship alongside advisor and protector. Not that I *need* protection, but it's nice to have backup all the same.

"Tell us another one, Blaize," I say, taking another sip of wine. I'm pacing myself, enjoying taking it slow. Plus, the way these males make me feel has my head spinning enough as it is. "I want more adventures of Blaize and Steel," I continue, and a small smile shapes his lips. The stories he's recanted tonight have truly helped whisk all of us away from the reality of our situation, taking us back to a nostalgic time of peace and mischief.

Blaize shifts on the cushions, resting his forearms on his knees, and I try to hide my stare behind my wine glass. Because *stars,* the warrior is gorgeous, the kind of beauty you know is deadly but can't resist. The silver on his one exposed arm almost shimmers in the candlelight that fills the room, the small red star looking like a drop of blood among the silver ink.

"I'm running out," he says, contemplative.

"What about the time Steel was caught naked in Emerald Lake?" River suggests, and I arch a brow between them.

"Steel, naked? Please, *do* tell," I say, and Blaize cocks a brow at me, a warning in his eyes.

"Careful, queen," he says. "I've never been jealous of Steel before, but if you keep looking like that when you say his name, I might be."

A lick of flame caresses my skin at the warning and I take another quick drink of my wine.

Blaize smiles, as if he's content with my reaction to his demands. "When we were younglings, barely thirty, Steel and I got into some trouble in the Earth Realm." My eyebrows raise at the mention of what used to be my home. "His father had sent Steel and his brothers out there for training and to learn the history of the realm, and naturally, I went with him." His eyes trail to the side as he recalls the memory. "Steel and I snuck off after his brothers went to bed, found a little mountainside pub, and drank until we couldn't see straight. We got lost trying to find our lodging and found the Emerald Lake instead. A night swim seemed perfect at the time, so we shed our clothes and dove in..."

I gasp, knowing full well the history of Emerald Lake.

"Yep," he says, nodding with laughter in his eyes. "I saw the aleds first," he says, referring to the carnivorous creatures that populated the lake. "Told Steel to get the hell out of there as I swam for the shore, but he was dead set on grabbing whatever plant was glowing bright green on the bottom." He shakes his head, his black hair shifting across his forehead. "I had to dive back in and drag him to the shore, kicking and punching, right before one of the aleds tried to make his ass a snack." A rough laugh rumbles his chest, the sound warming my insides. "By the time I got him out of the water, his brothers had found us standing there stark naked. But Steel had the plant in his hands, not knowing he was allergic to it. Couldn't write to save his life for a week, his hand was swollen to twice its size."

I join his laughter, as does Varian and River. "This is too good," I say, feeling slightly bubbly from the drink and the company. I touch the center of my necklace, awakening CB-2 from his slumber.

The little robot vibrates to life as he slides off my neck, blinking the little blue eye at me. "Call Cari," I say, and he immediately obeys.

"Don't you dare!" Blaize says, reaching for the little hovering robot, who dutifully darts out of his reach.

Light illuminates from the center and seconds later, Cari is smiling in the middle of our room, Lock behind her, kissing her neck.

"Did you really just answer a call right now, darling?" Lock says from behind her, and I can't help but blush at the look he gives her.

"It's Gessi," Cari says. "I always answer for Gessi." Cari glances around the room, raising her eyebrows. "And River and Blaize and Varian, apparently."

Lock mumbles a hello, his large hands on Cari's arms as he goes back to kissing her neck.

"Having fun, Ges?" she asks, and I bite back my smile.

Right now, I am having fun and I'm not allowing myself to feel guilty about it.

"Oh, you have no idea," I say, grinning at my friend. I miss her so much. Blaize waves his arms at me in a *don't even think about it motion,* but I forge on. "Blaize here was just sharing the most interesting stories about one of your mates. Is Steel in the room by chance?"

"What?" Steel's voice sounds from somewhere distant in the room, but he quickly storms into view. Shirtless. Stars, Cari's mates are gorgeous. There is no denying that. But, with my assassins in the room, it's hard to give him the credit he likely deserves. No offense to the All Plane kings, but they have nothing on my Shattered Isle assassins.

"Blaize?" Steel asks accusingly.

Blaize clenches his eyes shut for a moment, and when he opens them again, they're on me—a promise of punishment that I'm not at all scared for. I'm excited, my blood racing at just the thought of him paying me back for this, and I can hardly breathe from the need building inside me.

"Something about an aled, a glowing plant, and being found naked at Emerald Lake," I say, only to rile Blaize up more. I like seeing this side of him, playful and promising and this side of dangerous.

Cari's brows raise as she looks at Steel. "Oh really? This sounds fun."

Lock pauses his kissing to laugh, and Cari's eyes go distant for a moment, like she isn't seeing us anymore but something else entirely.

A moment later, she bursts out laughing.

"Did you just show her, Lock?" Steel groans, silently cursing his brother's mind-penetrating powers. Lock merely laughs. "Blaize, what the hell, man?" Steel asks, but he's laughing too.

"Don't be upset, mate," Cari says, smoothing her arm over his chest. "You know I never can resist a chance to see you naked."

Varian nearly chokes on his wine. "Can we party like she does? Because, *yes*."

Lock's eyes snap to Varian's in a playful warning. "Don't make me slice up your mind, beast."

"Love to see you try, shadow spitter," he fires right back.

Steel points toward Blaize. "Next time we see each other, be prepared."

Blaize raises his silver arm toward him. "I'm always prepared, but I really would hate to beat you now that you're officially a king."

The smile they share is heartwarming, the sign of an unbreakable friendship that I recognize only because I have that with Cari.

"Miss you," Cari says to me, as if reading my mind.

"Miss you," I say.

"Everything else going okay?" she asks, and I move with CB-2 out of the sight of my assassins, and she does the same with her mates, much to their audible objections.

"Tonight, it is," I say. "I'm...allowing myself an escape tonight. I felt like I was going to break if I didn't," I admit. And in truth, I'm nowhere near close to wanting this night to end.

"I understand the feeling," she says. "Don't deny yourself anything that brings you joy, Gessi," she continues, glancing back behind her where I know two of her mates wait. "Those moments of joy are the ones that will keep you from breaking under the pressure in the end."

"I'll do my best," I answer.

"Call me anytime you need me," she says. "I know I asked a lot of you—"

"I don't resent your decision," I assure her. "I promise. I just...I'm still getting used to it. And with the general still on the loose..."

We both share a concerning look, but I quickly shake my head. "Not tonight. We'll worry about that tomorrow."

"Agreed," she says. "I can share news of our efforts here. Tomorrow." She grins at me, waggling her eyebrows. "For tonight, I'd suggest you get back to your own...escape."

I grin at her, breathing more deeply at the support and love from my best friend. "Love you," I say.

"Love you, too."

"Love you, Gessi!" Lock and Steel call in unison before CB-2 shuts down the call and hovers by my face, resting against my shoulder until I slide my fingers over him and he slips around my neck again.

I chuckle, looking back at where Varian, Blaize, and River are in deep conversation about something that sounds hilarious. Crane is near invisible in the corner and part of me wants to go to him, to finally let him speak all the truths he's been trying to lay bare, but I just don't have it in me. I don't want to cry and rage tonight. I want...

I want something *more*.

But if I ask for it, I know any one of them—or all of them —will give it to me without question. Because I'm their queen. And that doesn't seem fair.

So, instead of heading back to my seat among them, I flash them all one last look, and make the walk to my chambers alone.

6

GESSI

I'm too restless to sleep, so I change into some comfortable pajamas and park myself on the royal blue tufted velvet chaise lounge with a book. I try to make the words on the page make sense, but I'm struggling.

Every instinct in my body is shouting at me, berating me for not staying where I was, for not losing myself in my assassins, if only for a night. But how could I stay? How could I cross that line and go back to giving them orders and asking them to risk their lives for me every night after?

I couldn't, because I knew it wouldn't be just one night. Not with them. Especially not with Varian, who I've known my whole life. Even if we'd managed to keep our hands to ourselves after that *one* night years ago.

It had been a special night on the beach where we'd each escaped our curfew confines, and when Crane and Cari were busy arguing over the best bow designs, Varian and I were exploring the coves farther down the sandy beach. Then, somehow, we were exploring each other.

My skin feels too tight for my body as the memory slides over me, making me all kinds of hot despite wearing only a thin pair of silk shorts and an oversized shirt. The night breeze caresses my skin from the open double doors leading to the balcony across the spacious room—the room meant for Cari when she ascended, but now belonged to me.

I shove the memory away, but the need that's been building in my body for the past six weeks is at an almost painful high. I blame River and Blaize right alongside Varian. And Crane...well, I've always wanted Crane in a way he's never entertained. Even my hatred can't quell that madness.

I toss the book on the floor, unable to focus. Every time the hero walks on the page, I see River's face or Blaize's calculating winter eyes. I feel Crane's stealthy presence or taste Varian's lips.

Pathetic, that's what I am. Lusting after my own personal assassins. I know it's a line I shouldn't cross, me being their queen. Their every instinct is to bow to me. And I shouldn't *love* the idea of them bowing to me, but it stirs something carnal deep inside me I can't ignore.

Closing my eyes, I let my imagination wander. There is no harm in that, right?

River is there first. His charming smile, his jokes that keep me laughing when all I want to do is succumb to the overwhelming demands of my new position. I can almost smell his intoxicating scent of mandarin and sage, can almost feel his powerful hands as he slides them over my body.

My own hands create the path meant for him and I sigh as I touch my oversensitive skin, all the while wishing it was him. Stars, I bet he kisses like a dream, all joy and laughter and sunshine, my All Plane warrior. I graze my fingers over my nipple, wishing it was his mouth before dipping my hand lower between my thighs—

A knock on my door freezes me. My eyes snap open and I listen harder, wondering if I imagined it.

Another knock.

I bolt off the chaise, rushing to the door in a hurry. Has something happened? Has the general been found? Has there been an attack on another village?

The questions race through my mind as I make it to the door, because why else would anyone be knocking on my door just before dawn?

I throw it open, nearly breathless, and find River standing on the other side of it.

His eyes go wide at the sight of me, and I guess I can't blame him. I'm in barely-there silk pajama shorts, my auburn hair hanging in messy waves over my shoulders, hardly the image of the put-together queen I've been trying to portray the last few weeks. But, to be fair, I wasn't expecting him.

"Is everything all right?" I ask after he's stood there too long in silence. He doesn't look alarmed or worried, just...shocked.

He braces his arms on either side of the doorframe as if to keep himself from entering my room. Heat surges under my skin at the look in his eyes, the need churning there. Wait, does he feel it too? This unexplainable need to be near each other?

"Tell me to go," he says, his voice rougher than I've ever heard it.

"What?" I whisper.

He wets his lips, those eyes grazing the length of my body before meeting mine again. "Order me to leave, and I will."

I'm trembling now, something stretching taut between

us. "And if I invite you in?" I ask, my voice no more than a whisper.

River glances behind me, his eyes roaming over the chaise lounge, the bed, the opened double doors leading to my private balcony.

"What are you looking for?" I ask when he hasn't moved.

"Honestly?" he asks.

"Always."

"The best place to make you come, my queen," he says, his eyes gauging, questioning, as if I'll scold him for stepping over an invisible line that no longer exists for me.

Not with him.

Not tonight.

I step to the side. "Won't you please come in, River?"

He shudders, and in a blink, I'm in his arms, pressed against his powerful, muscled body. The leather from his suit rubs against my barely-there silk, and I gasp at the contrast. He kicks the door shut behind him at the same time his lips find mine.

His lips are sweet and sinful as he takes his time exploring my mouth. He slides his tongue against mine, tasting me in sipping kisses that have my heart racing. My body tingles from the way he's holding me against him, learning the curves of my mouth as he walks us farther into the room. I fist his shirt, my feet hardly touching the ground as we make it to the closest available surface—the chaise lounge I'd left moments ago.

"My queen," he groans between my lips, breaking our kiss as I fumble with his shirt, desperate to feel his skin on mine. "Tell me you want this. Tell me I'm not overstepping—"

"I want you, River. I want this, whatever it is. I *need* you."

"Thank the sun," he says, claiming my mouth again. "I

know I'm not supposed to want you this way, not supposed to cross this line with you. As your assassin, but..."

"You couldn't stay away?" I finish for him.

"Yes," he answers, staring down at me in wonder.

The connection between us perks up, like a purring cat begging for attention.

"Gessi," I say, and he tilts his head. I reach up on my tiptoes, kissing him again. Relishing his taste and the way I feel with his arms wrapped around me. "Not my queen. Not here. I want to be your...Gessi."

A smirk shapes his lips. "As long as I get to call you *mine*."

My heart soars at the verbal claiming and we collide in a tangle of tongues and teeth, our hands roaming, exploring, savoring.

I finally get his shirt off, his pants following soon after. I almost moan at the sight of him. He's carved muscle and smooth skin and my fingers shake as I explore the lines of his chest, his abdomen, then down to his considerable length. I wrap my fingers around his hard shaft, and he groans at my grip.

"Fuck, Gessi," he says, and I love the way my charming assassin sounds cursing.

He thrusts into my hand as he kisses me breathlessly, his hands slipping under my shirt, teasing my nipples until they're pert for him. He reaches for the hem of my shirt, moving to take it off, and I freeze—

"Wait," I say, and he immediately stops.

He takes his hands off me, stepping back enough that I lose my grip on him. "I'm sorry—"

"No," I cut him off. "I just..." I can't form my words. They're tangled in my throat. I know River won't mind my scars, the ones the general and Erix bestowed upon me, but...I'm not ready. Slowly, I slip my shorts down, letting them pool at my feet before I step out of them. "For tonight, would it bother you if I left my shirt on?"

Concern and support flash through his eyes. "Of course not," he says, stepping toward me again. "But I want you to know you're perfect to me. You have nothing to hide or worry about. Not with me."

My heart swells in my chest and I know he's not lying, but...

"I know that," I say, wanting him to know I understand. "It's for me. I'm sorry, I..."

A muscle in his jaw ticks as his eyes fall to the oversized shirt like he can see what's beneath. He slides his fingers into my hair, tipping my head to meet his eyes. "You never apologize. Not with me, you understand?"

I grin up at him. "Giving me orders now?"

He smiles back. "Maybe."

He cocks a brow, tilting his head to look down my body, still holding firm to my hair. With his free hand, he tentatively slides his fingers down my shirt and dips between my thighs.

I gasp at the contact, my eyes widening as he doesn't hesitate to slide his fingers through where I'm already wet and aching for him.

"Sun above," River hisses. "You're slick, Gessi. So fucking slick for me already." He kisses me, rough and hungry, before pulling back, still teasing me with his fingers. "What were you doing before I came in here?"

I reach up, wrapping my arms around his neck as I rock into his hand, urging him to move. "Thinking about you."

His entire body shudders and one second, I'm standing there, riding his hand unabashedly, the next, I'm perched on the edge of the chaise lounge and he's dropping to his knees before me.

"I'm always thinking about you," he says, slowly spreading my thighs. "Is this what you were imagining?" he asks, massaging my trembling thighs, each stroke going higher, teasing the spot I'm aching for him most.

"Yes," I say, my pulse pounding in my ears. The sight of him there, on his knees, looking at me like I'm the most delicious sweet he's ever tasted, is *doing* things to my body.

"And this?" he asks, planting a languid kiss to my inner thigh. I brace myself with one hand behind me and grip his hair with the other.

"Yes," I breathe the word, the anticipation inside me coiling like a tight spring. Everywhere he touches tingles beneath my skin, everywhere his lips meet is like a flame igniting.

"And what about this?" He kisses his way up my thighs until he reaches my center and slowly, so slow it almost *hurts*, he licks me.

My head falls back, warm chills erupting all over my skin from the carnal caress.

But he pauses, and I lift my head back up, the breath in my lungs tight with need.

"Tell me you want this, one more time," he says. "Because once I start, I will not stop until I've made you come so many times you won't be able to move without feeling me."

A shiver runs through my body at his promise. "I want this, I want *you*."

The words are his undoing because he lowers his head again and *feasts*.

"Oh my...stars," I gasp, my grip in his hair tightening as

he laps and sucks and swirls his tongue around that sensitive bundle of nerves.

"You taste like a dream," he says against my oversensitive flesh, and I rock upward, using my grip on his hair to grind against his mouth. "Fuck, yes," he groans. "Just like that, Gessi."

He pulls away, just enough to slide a finger inside me, flicking his tongue over my swollen clit as he plunges it in. I gasp, rocking into it, needing more, more, more. He slides another one in, filling me with his fingers and torturing me with his tongue. He pumps me, working me into a writhing mess as he sucks my clit into his mouth—

My body clenches around him as my orgasm tears through me, sending waves of pleasure rippling down my spine as I moan his name. The release has been weeks coming, the need of his hands on me stretching out like a tightrope until he gave me what I needed to snap.

Slowly, he pulls his fingers from me and shifts on his knees, hooking an arm around my back to lift me. I throw my arms around his neck as he spins me, laying me on my back until I'm stretched out over the chaise lounge.

And when he settles between my thighs, the head of his hard cock sliding through my wetness, I can barely breathe from the sensation of it all. He keeps himself hovering above me with the strength of one elbow braced near my head, our eyes locked, the passion and question still ringing there.

River, my friend, my assassin. He's still here, asking if I want this, even when I've already given myself to him. And maybe it's because he feels what I feel, that unexplainable thing inside me begging me to get closer, to not stop until we're joined in every way a being can be. Maybe he needs to know he's not alone in that feeling we can't shake.

"River," I whisper his name, reaching between us, fisting

his cock and lining it up with my entrance, the motion causing shivers to dance over my skin. I'm so sensitive, he's already made my world unravel with his mouth. I can't imagine what his cock will do.

"Fuck," he whispers, eyes clenching shut as I guide him in an inch. "You feel so good, Gessi," he says, taking over with my crystal-clear consent, inching himself in slowly until he's seated to the hilt.

His mouth finds mine—all hot and slow and claiming— as I adjust to the size of him. And once my body relaxes around his, I wrap my legs around his hips, and move him. He groans at the motion, letting me take control a few more times before he shifts, gripping the back of the chaise for leverage as he glides in and out of me.

I arch into him, digging my nails into his back as he finds a home inside me again and again. Every nerve in my body is awake, sparking to life in a way I've never felt before.

This is joy, this is bliss, this is pure, *primal* need.

He increases his pace, sliding his other arm beneath my lower back, lifting me higher to fuck me from a deeper angle—

I come again, moaning as my thighs tremble around him, my pussy clenching around his cock. I relax, breathing through the aftershocks, and find him smirking down at me.

"You don't think we're done here, do you?"

My eyes widen. "I don't know if I can handle anymore," I say, my body already trembling with sensation.

"Want to find out?"

I smile, eyes wild and astonished as I look up at him and nod.

"Hang on to me," he says, and I immediately lock my ankles around his back, my arms already around his neck. Our bodies are flush as he slams into me, harder than before, and I whimper at how good it feels. "You like that, don't you, my queen?" he asks, doing it again, harder this time. "You like the way my cock feels pounding into you."

His words are shocking and delicious, my charming, polite assassin talking to me like I'm no more than a common whore.

And I find I like it too.

I like it a whole hell of a lot.

"Yes," I say, moaning as he does it over and over again. Each time he slams home, he grinds against my overworked and swollen clit, the pleasure building inside me sharp and bordering on an exquisite, addictive pain.

"Gessi," he says, and the intensity in his voice jolts through me, snapping my eyes to his. He doesn't stop moving, doesn't stop fucking me relentlessly, but our eyes are locked and something shifts between us.

That connection between us is no longer purring like a cat. It's an explosion of light and love and something ancient I don't understand and can't deny. A familiar power that is wholly new and somehow feels like I've always had room for it inside my body.

Not *it.*

Him.

River.

My heart yawns awake, shaking and trembling with life like I've never known. And River is there, a golden strand of power weaving around my soul.

Oh. My. Stars.

"*River,*" I say, tears springing to my eyes from how over-whelming the sensation is. He moves inside me, dragging himself all the way out and slamming home again, thrusting with powerful moves of his hips as he holds my gaze. "River, you're..."

"Mate," he says, breathless as he increases his pace. Driving into me so hard and fast, he sends me soaring, absolutely *soaring* over an edge I didn't know existed. I swear I see stars as I come again, this time in waves that spark with pain and pleasure and are so all-encompassing tears roll down my cheeks.

River groans, falling over that edge right alongside me, until we're both collapsing on the chaise, catching our breath. He rolls us to the side, positioning me half on his chest so he doesn't crush me. He runs his fingers through my hair, our sweat-slick bodies getting chills from the breeze through the opened doors.

"*Mate*," I say the word out loud and it only solidifies what is already sighing with relief inside me. The unexplainable connection, the sense of ease and trust that was so easily gleaned between us...River is my mate.

"Tor told me about how it feels," he says, shaking his head. "But it's so rare. I never thought it would happen to me."

My mind whirls with the odds and then I go straight into overthinking mode. Because that's what I do, and I've felt this connection before. Which means...

I bite my lip and shift to look up at him. "Are you upset about the bond?"

He furrows his brow. "How could I be, when I'm lucky enough to be mated to you?"

Relief slides warm and sweet over my body. "But you know what this means," I say. True bonded mates are rare in our realms, but they never come in just one pair. Like Cari and her All Plane kings. And if what I felt with River is any indication, I have an idea who might be my others.

"I do," he says, smiling down at me. "I can share if you can," he says, and the thought has me arching against him on instinct. The idea of River and me and someone else has my body heating in all sorts of ways that shouldn't be possible after what he just did to me, but I can't stop it. "Oh, you *like* the idea of that, do you, my queen?" he shifts, kissing me up and down my neck, my shirt sticking to my body from the heat he keeps creating.

"Maybe," I say, kissing him back.

He looks down at me, an easy, effortless smile on his face. "What can I do for you now, my queen?"

I tremble in his embrace. "Kiss me until the sun goes down," I beg.

And he obliges.

7

GESSI

"River?" Cari says, her tone pitching as she bounces up and down. CB-2 mimics her movements as he keeps us connected.

I bite back my smile, nodding at her from where I sit on my bed.

River left for his own chambers an hour ago, reluctant but duty-bound with his nightly routines as my assassin— perimeter checks, assessing threat levels from any recent messages received, and strategizing new defensive techniques should we ever face an attack. And after all that is done he's taken it upon himself to update the palace's technology with all his knowledge and talent from the All Plane.

"You're mated to River," Cari says again as if she can't believe it. Her eyes light up. "How are you feeling about it?"

"You know exactly how it feels," I say, my heart fluttering in my chest at the mere thought of my mate.

My mate.

I never thought I'd get so lucky to find one, let alone...

"What's wrong?" Cari asks, reading the conflict on my face.

"The connection I feel with him," I say almost timidly. "The one I've been trying to figure out since he arrived?" She nods, urging me to continue. "I've felt it before. It's not the same—it's entirely different really—but...the intensity, the unexplainable need, it's there."

Cari's lips part. "With who?"

I swallow hard, shifting on my bed.

"Why do you look worried?" she asks.

And her question is valid. It's normal for mates to come in threes, sometimes fours in our realms.

"It's not just *one* other," I say, my heart clenching. Anger burns through me as I flash through decades of memories. Decades of feelings and longing and all the things I could never have.

"Crane," Cari says, sympathy flashing through her eyes. She can likely guess the other I'm referring to, but she doesn't say his name out loud. "Ges, if that's true..."

"It can't be," I quickly say, even though my heart is begging to differ. "It can't be. If he was my mate, he'd feel it too. And leaving me locked in that dungeon..."

Memories snake into my mind, the scars along my torso and chest pricking against the thoughts.

"Have you spoken to him about it?" she asks.

"He's tried, but I can't, Cari. I can't. The memories haunt me enough, sometimes stealing my concentration when I'm trying to run our queendom. Hearing his excuses...what could possibly erase the pain he's caused?"

"I don't know," Cari says. "But I understand. If you're not ready, you're not ready. Don't do things on his timeline to ease *his* guilt. Do things on your own terms when you know it will help heal you the most."

"Have I told you that I love you?" I ask, sighing in the relief from her support.

"Many times. And I'm truly glad to hear it. I figured you'd hate me after I put such a massive responsibility on you."

"Never," I say.

"What am I supposed to do about the others?" I ask. "What if my instincts are wrong? Should I just ignore it?"

Cari laughs lightly. "Those instincts are hard to ignore. Trust me. I was sent to kill my mates, remember? And look how that turned out." She flinches at the mere mention of harming her mates, and I completely understand. The idea of River getting hurt...it's enough to make my stomach turn.

Fast. This is all happening so damn fast.

"How can I go from just enjoying him as my friend to being so irrationally possessive of him in the span of a night?"

"That's what happens when you accept the bond," she says, something glittering in her eyes—likely the memory of her own bonds with her mates.

"Sex," I say, and she blurts out a laugh. "That's the key to knowing for sure?"

"Yes," she says. "Something that harkens back to the primal days in ancient times. Consummating the bond is the only proper way to tell if the connection you feel is a true bonded mate or merely fantastic chemistry. You knew easily enough with River, right?"

I nod. The moment he'd touched me in that way, I'd felt it building and then when he slid inside me, claimed my body, he'd claimed me as his. A proper match, a true bonded pair.

"So you know what you need to do if you want answers to the questions distracting you," Cari says, and my eyes snap to hers.

"You're suggesting..." My voice trails off as images fill my mind, making my body hot all over again.

"Sleep with them. All of them. Whoever you have even the slightest inkling might be your mate."

I laugh, the mere idea of it spinning my head. "You're serious?"

"Absolutely. Finding my mates changed my life. I'm stronger because of them, happier. And if you sleep with them and don't find your true pairing, then at least you know and—judging by the looks of them—probably had fun finding out. What do you have to lose?"

"Nothing, I suppose," I say, shrugging. Because it's not like I'd *order* them to sleep with me. When the moment presents itself, I'll simply offer the situation and see what happens. Easy, simple. Right?

"Then what are you waiting for?" Cari teases, and I flash her a chiding look.

"I do have a queendom to run," I say, and she laughs.

"Don't we all," she says, sighing. "I love you," she continues. "Do whatever feels right. Life is too short to dwell in the realm of *what-ifs* and *should-I's.*"

"Love you too," I say, and we end the call. CB-2 nuzzles my neck until I pet him, shifting him back to the necklace around my neck.

I lay back on my bed, feeling lighter than I have in weeks, months.

I have the support of my best friend.

I have the love of my people, despite the tumultuous times we're trying to overcome.

I have a mate.

And I have the prospect of more...I just have to gain the courage to find out.

8

VARIAN

"Ah, look," I say as I clear the stairs to the outdoor training room that sits on the roof of the palace. "The pretty boy made it."

River cocks a brow at me. "You called for a training session at midnight, so here I am."

I stalk across the pristine black marble floor, the specks of sliver scattered across it flickering like stars. Stone tables line the exterior of the open room, littered with weapons ranging from throwing knives to blaster guns.

The rest of the space is wide open, with only a four-foot stone wall barricade separating the place from the four-hundred-foot drop to the ocean below. The night sky stretches wide above our heads, the midnight blanket clear and pristine as the moon casts everything in a slivery glow, and lit torches hang from sconces along the half-wall, spaced evenly apart to illuminate what the moon doesn't.

"But you don't look too happy about it," I say, once I've reached him. He's leaner than I am, but we see eye to eye. I motion to the purple spreading beneath his eyes. "In fact, you look downright exhausted."

Blaize saunters in behind me, coming to stand on my right side as he scans River's face too. "You look like shit," he says, and River rolls his eyes.

"Is this part of the training?" River asks. "Because if so, I'm not into it." He folds his arms over his chest, then nods to Blaize. "How come you look so refreshed?"

"Because I wake up for four hours every day and spend it in the sun," Blaize answers, and River drops his arms, shock coloring his eyes. "Have you not been doing the same?"

"No," he says, and I can hear the exhaustion in his tone.

"Isn't that like...essential for you sun worshipers?" I tilt my head at him, something twisting in my gut at the idea of him not taking care of himself. I shake it off, furrowing my brow at him. If he dies in battle because he's being reckless with his energy stores, then so be it.

"Why didn't you tell me?" River asks.

Blaize shrugs. "I figured you were doing it on your own," he says. "Besides, this is the most we've spoken in decades. Don't pretend like we're friends."

A muscle in River's jaw ticks. "We're on the same side," he says. "Even more now than we were at home. We protect our queen. I'm willing to put the past in the past if you are." He extends his hand toward Blaize, and I feel like I need a snack as I watch all this drama unfold.

I lean in close to River, my eyes dancing between him and Blaize's stare down. "What happened between you two?"

Blaize huffs a laugh, still not taking River's hand. "This one has his head so far up Tor's ass that he hates me on principle."

"I don't hate you," River snaps.

"But you have your head up Tor's ass?" I ask.

River glares at me. "No. And no more than you do Steel's," he throws at Blaize. "If you hadn't openly defied every order King Augustus delivered—"

"The traitorous king, you mean?" Blaize cuts him off, shaking his head. "Seriously. You can't throw that in my face anymore. Not after what came to light. He was a sadistic asshole who was content to murder Lock because he found out the truth. And Steel and Talon and Tor were next."

"Fine, fair enough. But before that. Before you knew—"

"I *always* knew," Blaize says.

"Then why didn't you tell anyone?" River challenges, finally dropping his hand.

Blaize grabs it, jerking him closer so they're eye to eye and look ready to rip each other's heads off.

Damn, where the hell is the snack I need? This is better than those plays the old king used to force us to watch. He'd made his elite assassins study the actors, made us learn their techniques so we could blend in to any situation without raising suspicion.

"I did," Blaize says, and River's lips part in shock. "I told Talon my suspicions years ago. Why do you think he hates me so much?" He grips River's hand harder, his muscles flexing as he squeezes, but River doesn't flinch, doesn't try to pull away. "Even now, he hates me because I saw what he couldn't. I *always* know when someone is disloyal."

"How is that?" I ask, genuinely curious.

"Just like you can shift into an obsidian beast," he says, then looks at River. "Just like he can create gadgets that can shrink his size or make things out of scrap metal in a matter of seconds, or my ability to always hit my target." He shrugs. "We just can."

I purse my lips, nodding. Interesting. Knowing if someone is disloyal or not is a pretty handy trick. I watch them, their hands still clasped, the sound of pops echoing between them they're both squeezing so hard.

"So, this is what's considered training now? Hand holding?" Crane's voice comes from the barricade a few yards away. He's perched on the thin stone ledge, quickly leaping off of it and landing as silent as a cat before he stalks over to us.

"I want to start over," River says, the first to break the silent competition. "Forget our past. Our queen is the new future and her safety means everything to me."

"To *all* of us," Blaize corrects him.

I study River a little more closely, sensing a shift in him, in the way he says *our queen.*

"Then we need to trust each other," River says.

Blaize hesitates, a hard cut to his cold eyes. "I only trust one person other than me."

River sighs, shaking his head.

"But," Blaize continues. "I can play nice. Sometimes," he adds, a smirk shaping his lips before they both loosen their grip and actually shake hands.

They break apart, and I clap. "That was entertaining," I say, then point an accusing finger at River. "Now, all that talk about trust and you're keeping secrets from us."

River's head tips back, like he's searching the sky for some kind of exit or patience or both. "How can you tell?"

Crane furrows his brow, stepping toward us and closing our little circle we have going on here.

I jerk my head in Blaize's direction. "Like him," I say, tapping my temple. "I've got a knack for sniffing out secrets. Credit can go to my decades and decades of ripping people's fingernails out to get them to tell the truth." I shrug. "There is another reason you look so exhausted, isn't there, pretty boy?"

The moment his eyes practically *sparkle,* I know.

I don't know how I know, but I do.

And it stirs something up inside me...not jealousy, not exactly, but...

The feeling of being left out?

I shove that shit down, drawing up a mask of pure amusement.

"You naughty, *naughty* assassin," I tease him. "You took liberties with our queen?"

Crane stiffens where he stands at River's left, and my instincts have me stepping between them, doing circles around River as the other two back up.

"I didn't take liberties," River says, his eyes following me as I circle him as if I'm some sea creature sizing up a meal. "Gessi—"

"Oh, it's Gessi, now is it?" I ask. "Not, *my queen?*" He's always been the most formal of our little assassin group, and now suddenly he's calling my friend by her first name? "You *must've* gotten a good taste then."

"Varian," Blaize warns, as if he can see something or sense something in River that should worry me.

Well, fuck that. This is too much fun.

Blaize steps in front of Crane too, not casually at all.

I stop circling River, stepping into his space so I'm all he can see. I lower my voice, an unchecked *something* pulsing in my gut. "Just always remember, I got there first. I'll always own a piece of her you never will—"

River slams into me, so fast he takes me down to the floor, his hands on my throat. I laugh—a booming, chest-shaking laugh—as he squeezes just enough to hurt not to kill.

"She's my *mate,*" he hisses the words, his eyes fury filled and this side of passionate. Fuck, I kind of like this look on the polite, charming, All Plane warrior.

Mate.

Mate.

The word clangs through me, sizzling on the edge of pleasure and pain. River is on top of me, hand wrapped around my throat, eyes primal as he lays claim to Gessi.

My Gessi.

"The fuck you say?" Crane snaps from somewhere behind us, drawing River's attention enough for me to gain the upper hand.

I shift my right arm, the monster beneath my skin rippling as the transformation comes in a blink, and I wrap my moldable black arm around his neck, like a tentacle drawing in its prey. River's boots dangle off the ground as I lift him, snarling at him as the monster surges to the surface.

Blaize is holding Crane back, the two descending into an all-out brawl.

River doesn't struggle, doesn't grab for my substance wrapped around his throat. Instead, he reaches beneath it, pressing something on his red suit—

He disappears.

I shift my arm back to normal as I whirl around, searching—

A sharp hit cracks my jaw so hard I'm thrown off my feet, my back snapping against the marble, the momentum sliding me backward a few feet.

I roll over, spitting blood on the pristine floor as I gather to my knees. A laugh rips from my chest as another hit lands on my gut, knocking me back over.

"Tiny assassin," I spit out, laughing as I leap to my feet.

The shift comes quickly, a hot sort of ripping sensation as I fully transform into the monster I've always been. My muscles quadruple and ripple beneath the black substance that makes me moldable, stretchable, and near indestructible, and my eyes turn thermal. "There you are," I growl, my shifted lips working around the razor-sharp teeth that fill my mouth.

I spot River—his red and yellow image no bigger than an ant—bouncing and racing toward me for another hit. One swing of my hand has him flying across the training floor, hitting the barricade so hard the stone cracks and crumbles around him.

He flickers back to his normal size, gripping his side. I extend my arm toward him, gently helping him to his feet before I swing that same arm at Crane and Blaize.

"Enough," I say, my voice garbled in this form.

Blaize and Crane are bleeding and bruised from the fight, just like River and me. Well, at least we're sharing now.

When they each calm down and walk toward me, I shift back to my normal form, the sensation like pulling off a ridiculously heavy coat.

"Now," I say, eyeing each of them. "Is this really how we want to behave? Like animals?"

"You're one to talk," Blaize says, but there is fire in his usually cold eyes. I get that. A good brawl can thaw even the iciest spirit.

"Fair enough," I say. "Like it or not, we're in this together. Like River said, we're all here for the same thing. To protect Ges. To be whatever she needs us to be. And I know her a little better than you—"

Crane gives me a murderous look, so I quickly amend, waving an arm between us. "*We* know her better than you two," I correct, and that appeases him a little. "I know she wouldn't want us tearing each other's throats out."

I eye Crane, who looks the most betrayed out of all of us. Though, to be fair, Blaize doesn't look thrilled either. I don't know if that's because he wants Gessi intimately or what, but either way, it isn't up to us. It's up to Gessi and the stars who create the bonds.

And you know what the stars want.

The voice in the back of my head echoes and I shove it down like I usually do. I've known what the stars have wanted from me for over a decade, but I haven't stepped a toe in that direction. Not when she's never expressed the same feeling. But lately, things *have* seemed different between us, and I wonder...

Not the time.

Right.

"Can we work together?" I ask. "We could all use a bit of training. If we're going to beat the shit out of each other, let's do it for the right reasons."

River laughs, and it breaks the tension between each of us. Crane still looks like he'd enjoy sending an arrow through River's eye, but even he's sane enough to understand that Gessi chose him, found him worthy.

And honestly, isn't that what any of us can hope for? To have a female as smart and funny and ruthless as Gessi to find them worthy?

My gut twists with memories, and I have to wonder if I've wasted too much time waiting for her to figure out what she wants. What if she never knew her options in the first place?

"I'm with River," Blaize says quickly, as if he's worried Crane will want to train with him, and I nod.

"That leaves me and you," I say, and Crane rolls his eyes.

"We know each other's moves by heart," he says, but squares up anyway.

"Never hurts to test it," I say, shifting into my monster form. "Come on," I growl. "Work off some of that anger. I can take it."

Crane flashes me an appreciative look, then punches me hard enough to break bone.

FOUR HOURS AND A SHOWER LATER, I slip into some loose black pants and a white sleeveless top, ready to collapse on my bed. Training had been unforgiving and relentless earlier, but fuck, we'd all needed it. Even Crane looked lighter as we went our separate ways, me to the assassins' chambers in the lower levels of the palace, and Blaize and River heading off to talk about the best times for sun absorption.

I stretch out on my bed, groaning at the deep pull my muscles need, but something unfurls inside me, a different kind of pull I know all-too-well.

Gessi.

She's close, but why?

I leap off the bed, rushing toward my door as I hear footsteps hurrying down the hall. I throw open the door, craning my head both ways, and spot just the ends of a flowing red dress around the corner.

"Ges!" I say, jogging down the hall to catch her.

I hear her stop just as I come around the corner. "What the hell are you doing down here?" I ask, my brow pinched. Not that there are any assassins left down here but me—all the others elected to take Ges up on her offer to find more suitable rooms elsewhere in the palace.

Not me though. I'm a monster, I know that, just like I

know where I belong. Staying down here has always helped me keep away from Ges...but now she's come to *me*.

"I..." Gessi opens her full lips, then closes them.

I take the time to trail my eyes over the length of her body. The dress covers her entirely, from her neck to her wrists, and is tight around her generous hips before flowing out and down to her ankles. My cock twitches with how mouthwatering she looks and how close she stands. She looks like a piece of forbidden fruit among the dark, dank stone walls that make up the assassins' quarters.

"You...what, Ges?" I ask, my voice low as I step closer to her.

She backs up until her spine kisses the wall, her head tilted back to hold my gaze.

I don't stop, unable to resist the pull. Usually I can. Usually I remind myself of all the reasons I've stayed away, but tonight something is different. Maybe I *am* a little jealous of River or maybe I'm just tired of pretending to not care. Either way, I brace an arm on the right side of her head, caging her in.

"I heard about the training session," she blurts out, her chest rising and falling a little faster. The motion has just the tips of her breasts grazing my chest, and it makes me even harder. Fuck, she smells like a dream and is so close, so delicate, like the flowers she creates.

"Pretty boy tattle on me?" I smirk.

"No," she says. "He just told me about it. He actually said you all seemed...to work well together after a while."

"And you came all the way down here to...what? Tell me I did a good job rallying our band of misfits? Or did you want to see how I'd react to the news of River being your mate?"

Gessi narrows her gaze. "Is that so bad? That I'd want to know what my friend thinks about it all?"

I grin down at her. "I only want you to be happy, Ges," I say honestly. "But you and I both know, just because he's your mate, doesn't mean you're *only* his."

She shivers against the wall.

"Was there something else you wanted?" I ask, not moving.

"I wanted..." Her eyes flicker from mine to my mouth and back.

"What?" I ask when she doesn't continue. "What did you want?" There is barely any space between us now, and she's looking up at me with nothing but fire and need in her eyes. I shift on my feet, the motion bringing my thigh between hers, and she gasps. "What really had you venturing all the way down here, only to run away before knocking on my door?"

Fuck, I want her to say it. I've always *wanted her to say it. But she's never, not once, come looking for me. Not again. Not after.*

Her pulse quickens, and I zero in on the sight. Stars, I'd love to bite that soft patch of skin on her neck. Love to taste the sounds of her moans on my tongue again.

"Tell me you never think about that night," I whisper, my free hand grazing over her shoulder and down to her wrist. She trembles beneath my touch, and everything in me reaches for her, everything I've always tried to keep buried. Not only because she's never shown any interest since, and I knew I wouldn't survive that kind of rejection, but also because the general. If he knew I had a weak spot, one like Ges? He would've exploited it. The king too.

But here? Now?

Ges is opening up more to me than she ever has before,

and we've barely spoken. But I can *feel* it, almost as if she's finally reaching back for me in the way I've always reached for her.

"I think about it," she says, arching her body as I move my thigh between hers, making her gasp with the contact.

"Which part do you think about most?" I ask, moving my free hand to her ribs, lightly grazing down to her hip and settling my hand there.

Fuck, I want to sink into her. I want to touch her and taste her again. I want her to feel what she does to me. Want her to know she's always been my undoing.

She wets her lips, and it takes everything in my power to remain still, to not lean down and suck that tongue into my mouth until she whimpers.

"Your mouth," she finally whispers, as if saying the words out loud will condemn us both. But we're no longer under anyone's rule. We no longer have to fear the king or the general using our bond to rip us apart, to weaken us. The only one capable of drawing lines now is *her*. "Your teeth," she says, and I shudder against her. "The way you felt against me, in me."

"Fuck, *Ges*," I groan, the memories from that night sizzling across my brain. I have it memorized. Every sound she made, every flavor she burst on my tongue. All of it. It's been my one escape amid the general's insufferable demands.

I tighten my grip on her hip, and she arches against me.

"Do you...think about it?" she asks, and I hate the doubt in her eyes.

"Are you kidding?" I ask, shaking my head. "It's all I've thought about. *You're* all I've thought about."

"Why didn't you tell me?" she asks, eyes filling with emotion.

"Why didn't you?" I ask, our mouths only inches apart.

"I asked you first," she says, and I smirk at her stubbornness.

"I knew from the second I sank into you, Ges. You were mine. Made for me. But...when you acted like nothing happened between us the next night, when you went back to behaving just like the friend I'd always had, I assumed you didn't feel the same. And I would not force you to love me, not when you're *you* and I'm nothing but a monster the general enjoyed setting loose—"

Her mouth steals the words from my lips, the kiss almost timid as her soft lips explore mine. She pulls back, her eyes gauging my reaction as her palms flatten against my chest.

"I thought you didn't want me," she says. "I thought I wasn't good enough, experienced enough—"

It's my turn to crush my mouth against hers, and this time, there is nothing timid about it. I sweep into her sweet mouth with my tongue, savoring the taste of her as I hike her leg around my hip. She whimpers in my mouth, grinding against my hard cock as she kisses me back.

"Fuck," I hiss between her lips. "*Ges.*"

She wraps her arms around my neck, pulling herself up enough to lock her ankles behind my back as I break our kiss to work my way up her neck. Supporting her with one arm under her luscious ass, I use my free hand to slide under her dress, dipping between her thighs. I push the scrap of lace covering her to the side and glide my fingers through her heat.

"Fuck, Ges. Look at you. All slick and hot for me."

She moans, rocking against my hand without hesitation. "I've been waiting a long time," she says. "I've always been ready for you."

Stars. My knees almost buckle at her words, but I keep

us upright, planting kisses up her neck as I tease that swollen bud with my fingers in tight circles.

"Varian," she says as I work her into a writhing mess. There is a warning in her tone, a desperation that completely matches mine. There will be time for exploring and teasing later. We've waited too long and now that she's openly said she wants this? I'm fucking done holding back.

I leave her sweet, wet pussy only long enough to push down my pants, just enough for my cock to spring free.

"Yes, please," she moans as I rub it between her slick heat. She rocks against me, coating me with her arousal, and I have to hold on tighter to keep from slamming home inside her.

"Bed," I growl. "I should take you to the—"

"Varian," she groans, a demand in her tone. "Fuck me. *Now.*"

And it's my undoing.

I thrust my cock inside her at the same time I clamp my teeth down on that sensitive flesh just below her jaw.

She moans, her pussy clenching around my cock as I thrust in again, biting her just a little harder this time.

"Fuck," I groan, pumping into her, shifting so both my hands are filled with her ass. I use that leverage to hold on to her, fucking her relentlessly against the wall.

Her thighs squeeze my hips so tight a ripple of pain shoots across my body, making me thrust harder, and her moans echo in the hallway like the best music in the realms.

She's slick as I glide in and out of her. Each time I slam home I make sure I hit her clit, giving her all the pressure she needs, pushing her right up to that edge I know she loves to dance on. The one where my teeth leave marks on her lush jade skin, the one where my cock buries so deep inside her she can't walk without feeling me there.

"Varian," she moans, and the sound of my name on her tongue while I'm seated to the hilt inside her has my soul stretching and tightening, reaching and pulling.

Braiding with hers.

"Do you feel that?" she asks, and I pull away from her neck until we're eye to eye.

I slow our momentum down, the pace almost torturous as I feel her pussy fluttering around me.

"Yes," I say. "I feel it." I hold her gaze, fear threatening to steal this perfect moment of bliss from me. She can reject me, reject the bond I've kept buried for years. It's all on her, because I've belonged to her from the moment she kissed me all those years ago.

"Do you want it?" she asks, and I shudder. "Do you want this? Want me? Forever?"

"How can you ask that?" I thrust into her hard enough to make her eyes roll back. "You're perfection. You're my best friend. You've always been mine, Ges. The question is, do you want me to be yours?" I hold us there, the anticipation straining between where our bodies are joined. "You know me, the monster I become. You know I can shift even if I have a nightmare. I'm dangerous. I understand if you don't want that chained to you forever." It would hurt like hell, but I would understand.

Tears well in her eyes and she lowers her head, slanting her mouth over mine in a possessive, claiming kiss. "I've never been afraid of you, Varian," she says. "And *always*," she continues. "I've always wanted to be yours."

Elation becomes a living, breathing thing inside me, climbing and building so much I can barely speak around it.

"Say it again," I demand, pumping into her hard and fast.

"I'm yours," she gasps, her nails digging into my back as

her pussy tightens around me. Our souls braid and intertwine with our dual consent and acceptance of the bond, and I feel like I'm being rebuilt from the inside out. "I'm yours, I'm..." Her words break off into a moan and she shivers around me as she comes, taking me right over the edge with her.

She collapses against me, her head dropping over my shoulder. I adjust our position, carefully carrying her into my room, where I gently clean us up.

"Mate," I say the word out loud, just because I need to know it's real, that this isn't all some cruel dream and that I'll soon wake up alone and cold in my dungeon of a room.

Gessi tucks into my side on my bed. "Mate," she says. "I can't believe we wasted so much time."

I look down at her. "I'll spend the rest of forever making up for that lost time."

She bites her lip, a mischievous grin there. "And River?"

"Good thing I'm fond of him." Heat slices through my veins. "We'll join him later. For now?" I lean down, kissing her again. "I want you all to myself."

9

GESSI

Two mates.

I have two mates.

The knowledge has me living in a blissful sort of glow these last two days. Even the people who come to request for help or services have noticed the change in me, showering me with compliments as we work to assist the cities and villages in need.

"Thank you," a harvester says to me now, bowing lower than she needs to while I sit on my throne in the public throne room.

"Please," I say, motioning for her to stand. "There is no need to inspect my floors," I continue with a smile. "I assure you, they're quite clean."

The harvester laughs. "I'm just so grateful, your highness. The additional hands will make our productivity triple."

"It should've been granted to you the first time you requested additional aid," I say, my jaw clenching. The general had denied her on the king's behalf, or perhaps it was his own. It was always hard to tell where King Jerrick's plots began and General Payne's ended.

She nods, her eyes flashing to the males standing stoically by my side. River and Varian on my right, Blaize and Crane on my left. It's a sight to behold, I'm sure, and I'm not unaware of how lucky I am to be protected and advised by such formidable and gorgeous males—let alone be connected to them in the way that I am.

Blaize casts me a sideways glance, the look I've come to know well these past weeks during the meetings with my people—it's time to move on to the next.

I sigh, but give the harvester my best smile and well wishes before she leaves and the next inquirer enters.

I don't enjoy keeping a time limit on conversing with my people, and while River or even Varian would likely indulge my need to let the people speak with me as long as they wish, Blaize is not so easily swayed. He's created a schedule that allows me to see at least fifty people a day—should there be that many in need, which there have been lately.

When we first started, I was barely making it through ten because I would hug and cry with them through their stories of hardship. Blaize never faulted me for it exactly, but he didn't pull any punches when it came down to the cold hard logistics either.

In fact, Blaize *never* pulls any punches with me. He's the only one of my assassins who doesn't treat me like glass. Sure, they all know how powerful I am, but whenever the memories of the past steal my breath and my focus, Blaize is the only one who doesn't coddle me. He pushes me, taking me right up to the edge of anger instead of pity, and I truly love that about him.

Not that I don't *love* River and Varian's methods of

comforting me, but it's a beautiful contrast that I don't understand how I'm lucky enough to deserve.

Crane, of course, always loves to argue with me or give me the silent treatment, but even he treats me like I'll break at any moment. His protective instincts over me now are almost suffocating, and yet those instincts were nowhere to be found when I *needed* them most.

The scars beneath my gown prickle with the memory and I shift on my throne while I listen to the next person's request.

Several hours later, I've just finished addressing the last request of the day, and I'm more than ready to grab River and Varian and drag them back to my chambers. We still haven't crossed the lines of all three of us being together, but I've noticed a friendship forming between them ever since Varian and I accepted our mating bond. They spend more time together even when I can't be with them—lunches and training and I even caught River showing Varian all the new tech he's outfitted the palace with. It makes my heart warm that they get along so well, and the idea of both of them together...

"Your highness," Lance hurries into the throne room, the panicked look in his eyes making me sit up straighter.

"What's happened?" I ask, alarmed to see him so rattled. Lance is usually calm and collected, ever the loyal leader of my new Shattered Isle guard.

"There has been another attack," he says, his tone strained. "We just got word from the sleeper drones King Talon left with us." He digs something from his pocket, pressing a button on a small device. The space before him lights up with images, much like CB-2 does when I call Cari.

I rise from my throne, my lips parted on a gasp as I descend the stairs to get closer.

"Is that the Slate Lands near the Onyx City?" I ask, unable to tell for sure from the gruesome images being shown. There is too much smoke, too much fire, too many screams ringing out among the wreckage.

"Yes, your highness," he says, clicking another button that speeds up the scene taking place in front of me. He stops it entirely when a certain individual crosses the path of the drone recording the footage.

"General Payne," I say, spitting out his name as my lip curls up.

Ice stings my veins as he stops in the middle of the carnage and looks up, directly into the drone's line of sight. I feel his eyes on me like the bony fingers of death, and when he points at the drone, showing off his razor-sharp teeth, I know the threating look is meant for *me*.

The Slate Lands on the northwestern side of the Isle are openly supportive of both myself and Cari, just like the fishing village was, and he's slaughtering them for it.

A weight settles on my chest that River and Varian must feel because they both take a few steps closer to me, as if to catch me if I faint.

"You're not going to let him get away with this, are you?" Blaize asks, and River immediately sends him a warning look. Blaize merely shrugs. "This has to stop. One way or another."

"Tact," Varian snaps. "Find it."

"No," I say, waving off River and Varian, who look ready to tackle Blaize. "He's right. This has to stop. I have to do something—"

"You can't," Crane says, shaking his head.

I glare at him, but there is barely any bite to it. I'm worn thin from him always opposing my ideas or my needs and now it just makes me feel...empty.

"She can," Blaize argues before I can. "She's not a break-able doll. This is her queendom—"

"And who do you think will rule the Shattered Isle if she leaves the throne vulnerable to attack? Don't you realize that's what General Payne wants?" Crane shifts on his feet, stepping into Blaize's space. "I've known the general since before I can remember," he says. "He enjoyed using King Jerrick as a puppet for his schemes, but always longed for the throne himself. Now he believes he has a chance and you want her to abandon the throne?" The threatening cut to Crane's sharp eyes has something inside of me waking up and growling.

"Stand down, Crane," I command, putting every ounce of authority I have into the tone. He flinches, blinking at me in shock. "Threatening one of my assassins is grounds for me to put you on your ass. And, as you know very well, I *can*."

Crane takes a step back, then another, and the tension in my chest eases the farther he moves away from Blaize. Once the anger has settled, I'm back to feeling...exhausted. I'm bone-weary exhausted from the back and forth between us. I miss the way things used to be.

I miss the friend who played cards with me, who would silently walk the beaches with me while Cari and Varian trained. I miss the friend who would complement my flowers and the friend who would let me tend to his wounds from training.

I span the distance between us, suddenly needing to see what's left of my old friend in his eyes. "Why can't you be on my side, Crane? Why have you stayed if you hate every deci-sion I make so much?" I ask, my voice lowered between the two of us.

He visibly swallows, and there is such devastation in his eyes. "I am on your side," he says. "Always and forever. I've never *not* been."

Tears well in my eyes, but the rest of the males in the room give us the space we need. "You defy me, you threaten your partners in the elite assassin guard, and you...you..." I blow out a breath.

"Ges, please. Let me talk to you. Let me tell you the truth," he begs.

"We have more important things to discuss right now," I say, unable to let my heart get shattered more than it already has. Besides, if he agrees to this, if he's with me on this, then I will hear him out on the journey. I make that promise with my soul and somehow feel strengthened by the internal decision.

I turn back to face the other males in the room. "Lance," I say, clearing my throat of the emotion Crane has caused. "Will you protect my people while I'm gone?"

"With my life," he immediately answers.

"Gone?" Crane asks.

Blaize gives me the smallest, almost imperceptible smile, and I swear pride flickers in his wintry eyes.

"Yes, gone," I say to Crane, then focus back on Lance. "I'll need you to protect not only the people, but my queendom, my throne. I trust you to make decisions in my place."

"Of course," he says, laying his hand over his chest. "General Payne will not breech these walls as long as I'm alive."

Pride swells in my chest, and I give him a grateful smile. "Good," I say. "Now that it's settled, I'll also need you to send a group of your royal guards to the northeast, toward the Cave Lands. I want you to inform them they'll be protecting the queen on a specialized journey. My sky-ship will be among them, but they'll need to be ordered not to disturb me while in transit." I cringe at the last part, but it's the only way my plan will work.

"Your majesty?" Lance asks, knowing there is something wrong with my tone.

"I won't be in the sky-ship," I clarify. "But I need your assassins to think I am. Spread the news through the royal city, and the surrounding villages as well."

"Clever queen," Blaize says, and a drop of golden warmth slides down the center of me at his praise.

"Where are we headed, then?" Varian asks, stepping close enough that his arm brushes mine. I breathe easier at the connection, the support from my mate. River is not far behind him, coming up on my other side as I ask Lance to switch the device to show a map of the Shattered Isle.

"We'll be heading here," I say, pointing toward the Salt Mines, a village close to the Slate Lands. I trace the path with my finger. "Because if General Payne hears of my journey *here*," I say, pointing toward the Cave Lands. "And he's just left there..." I say, pointing to the Slate Lands.

"Then he'll most likely be intercepted here, at the Nocturne Lands," Blaize finishes for me.

"Exactly," I say. "Our position from the Salt Mines will give us the advantage. We can sneak up on him from behind."

"That's a beautiful fantasy," Crane says, and I snap my eyes to his. "But you have no intel on the number of soldiers traveling with him. Plus, the fact that he can become invisible and has telekinetic powers makes him an even more formidable foe—"

"Do you even want me to catch him?" I snap.

"No!" he yells back.

I gape at him.

"I don't. I don't want you anywhere near him!"

"Careful," River warns. "Your tone leaves a lot to be desired."

"I don't give a fuck," Crane snaps. "She shouldn't be anywhere near the general ever again, and you know it. As her mates, you two should argue this side, not me."

Something sharp pierces my chest and I don't know if it's his clear opposition to my idea or if it's because he's yelling at my mates to talk sense into me, but fuck, it *hurts*.

"She deserves to drive a poisonous barb straight through his heart," Blaize says. "And only her. He's *her* kill and you know it."

Crane looks at Blaize in disbelief. "You can't be serious—"

"He's right," I say, elation storming me at the idea of ending the general's reign of terror forever, with my own hands, my own powers. "General Payne is mine." I look directly at Crane, already fully aware that River, Varian, and Blaize are with me. "You can either come with us and support us or stay here and protect my isle. I honestly don't care anymore, Crane."

The words are like acid on my tongue because as much as I'd love for them to be true, they're a lie.

Because I *do* care.

More than I should.

More than makes sense.

But I do. I care so damn much it makes me sick. I'm hanging suspended in this moment, barely breathing as I wait for his answer. Somehow, it's vital to me, and I hate myself for placing so much importance on a male who clearly doesn't do the same for me.

I have the support of two amazing mates, and even

Blaize for stars' sake. Why does it matter to me so much that Crane is on my side?

"I'm with you," Crane finally says, and I shudder with relief. "This is suicide," he continues. "But I'm with you."

10

GESSI

"My sky-ship is faster," River says as he scans the small command room on Varian's personal vehicle.

It's small and discreet and exactly what we need for this journey.

"Faster isn't always better," Varian says, clicking a few buttons on the control panel, setting our planned coordinates and shifting it to autopilot. He glances over his shoulder at me, nothing but pure mischief in his eyes. "Isn't that right, love?"

Heat washes over my body, and I bite my lip to keep from smiling at the murderous look on River's face. I quickly raise my hands in defense as I back out of the command room. "I have no complaints with either of you."

I spin on my feet, hurrying down the hallway, laughter rising in my chest as the two of them continue to bicker back and forth. I turn the corner and immediately crash into Blaize.

"Sorry," I say, my palms flat on his broad chest.

He gently grips my arms, steadying me as he looks down at me.

"Don't apologize," he says, his voice low and rough like always, but something about the *command* in his tone has my body tightening with anticipation.

No one commands me anymore. I'm the queen of the Shattered Isle. He's one of my elite assassins. I rule over him, but somehow, he's always the one in charge.

And I'm pretty sure I like it.

"Do you like telling me what to do?" I ask, stepping out of his way.

He follows my path until my back presses against the wall of the hallway.

"I think the better question would be," he says, leaning over me with one arm braced on the wall. "Do you like doing what you're told?"

My breath catches as warm shivers dance over my skin. This feels like a game between us, but I have no idea how to win. The only thing I *do* know is that I don't want to stop playing.

I hold his gaze, marveling at the almost white streaks in his winter blue eyes. My heart pounds in my chest, my entire body hanging by a thread he controls. He drops his gaze, scanning the lines of my face, and lower, to the royal blue gown that covers most of my jade green skin. The reminder of *why* I constantly choose full-body gowns settles into my soul, cold and icy.

Blaize tilts his head, noticing the shift in me, and backs away a couple of steps. As if he thinks the reaction is because of *him,* because of how close he stands.

I part my lips, ready to explain, but Varian finds us. "Everything all right here, love?" he asks. I nod as Blaize makes his way past Varian, likely heading to the small seating area Varian's ship has. No doubt Crane is sulking in there as well. "We're about to land in the orchard village," he continues.

"Wonderful," I say, my breath still shaky from the moment with Blaize. The last thing I want is for him to think I'm afraid of him, but we have bigger things to worry about right now. I smooth out my gown despite its lack of wrinkles, using the moment to focus on what matters. "I'm ready."

Twenty minutes later, Varian's ship is docked on the outskirts of the orchard village, and my assassins follow me off of it.

"Your plan allows for this?" Crane asks from where he walks to my left, those sharp eyes scanning every inch before us and seeing farther than I'll ever be able to. There isn't any bite to his tone, but the question adds another weight to the already overwhelming number of weights he's placed on my chest recently. I'm not sure how much more I can take before I break.

"Yes," I answer, doing my best to breathe evenly. "You didn't reach the western side of the Isle when you were spreading the word about potential attacks. This isn't far from the Slate Lands. I won't fly over this village and leave it unprepared should the worst happen. Especially with the Slate Lands and Onyx City so close."

"I've gone over the logistics five times," Blaize adds from behind me. "We have at least five days before we'll intercept the general."

"And whatever army he has with him," Crane says. "If he's even still on the path we assume he is."

I hate that he isn't wrong. Hate that he's merely expressing all the doubts that are gnawing at the back of my mind. This plan may not work. It may be a total waste of our resources and time, and with the throne vulnerable, who is to say I've made the right decision?

Crane is merely expressing those concerns, those dangers. I know Varian and River and Blaize have thought of the odds too, but haven't been as bold as Crane to express them.

Doubt slithers through me as I question my actions for the millionth time since Cari named me queen. It doesn't matter what I do, someone will always be waiting for me to fail, waiting to steal the throne from me. Until I can prove to anyone who would challenge me that stealing from me isn't an option. Harming my isle isn't an option.

Killing the general and putting a stop to his vicious attacks would certainly prove that, so I shove the doubt down and forge ahead.

The orchard village is a bustling little town just off the coast of our beloved obsidian ocean and it is the principal supplier of fresh fruits throughout the Isle. The smell of citrus and the sea hangs in the air as we come to the central hub of the village, comprising a main street surrounded by quaint sandstone buildings painted in every color, from tangerine to sapphire.

Some locals carrying wares on the sidewalks lining the buildings spot us, their calm expressions quickly turning to shock before they bow. I swallow hard, still getting used to these reactions. Two months ago, I could've strolled through these streets with no one giving me a second glance.

Well, maybe they would have looked twice, since I'm an Earth Realmer who'd been raised on the Shattered Isle, but they certainly wouldn't have bowed.

Not that Cari's father ever allowed us that much free-dom, anyway. The only times we escaped the palace walls with his knowledge and approval was when he'd send Cari on missions across the Isle—some peaceful, some brutal. I was always there, traveling with her, ensuring she had whatever she needed to survive, whether that was food or clothes or the support of someone who loved her.

I run my fingers absently over my necklace, missing her. I've thought about calling her so many times to ask what she'd do in my position, but she has too much on her plate already. Plus, I want to prove to her that I can do this on my own. I want to make her proud.

"Your highness," a male says, approaching us and bowing low at the waist.

I smile at him, motioning for him to rise. He wears a colorful tunic embossed with fruit vine details and dons what I can assume is the badge of a leader on his right breast. "Are you Trince?" I ask, plucking the name from the Shattered Isle ledgers Cari had left for me to study, and his eyes light up.

"At your service, your highness," he says, bowing again before he glances at my assassins behind me. "Have we done something not to your liking? The last transport of fruit to the palace was some of our best."

Panic flickers over his features, punching me right in the chest. Fear ebbs off him in waves, and I shouldn't be surprised—Cari's father and General Payne did their best to rule with nothing but violence and fear. But I'm here to change all that.

"No, of course not," I say. "Your product is always stunning," I continue, and he visibly relaxes. "There are some important matters we need to discuss."

"Absolutely," he says, motioning toward the building he'd just come out of. "Please, join me."

I follow him inside the little sapphire building, the interior decorated in a clean and minimalist way with only the sparsest wooden furniture and shining stone floors. We settle at a small table with only two chairs, him on one side and me on the other. Blaize and Varian take vigil outside the building's doors, River and Crane content to watch me from the hallway.

"This is where I conduct all town matters," Trince says, motioning to the shelves of books and papers and artwork scattered about the room. "What is it we can do for you?"

"I need you to prepare for the possibility of an attack," I say, and his expression is blank for a few seconds before his eyes widen.

"An attack?" he asks, his voice cracking slightly. "Why would anyone attack our peaceful orchard?"

Something about his tone has me glancing at Crane, whose eyes are narrowed on Trince too.

"General Payne has been attacking randomly along the Isle since I took the throne," I explain, shoving away that odd, prickling sensation on the back of my neck. Trince runs a peaceful village. Of course he's acting skittish at the mere idea of an attack.

"We aren't warriors," Trince says, wringing his hands. "We don't have the means to defend ourselves against an attack from the general himself—"

"No one has those means," I say, and he nods quickly. "I'm actively working to stop the threat, but I want you to be prepared—"

"How?" he cuts me off, and my brows raise at the sharpness in his tone. "Forgive me, your majesty," he says, dipping lower in his seat. "I only mean...what can we do to protect ourselves?"

I take a deep breath, trying to put myself in his shoes. This evening he woke up and tended to his village as he's done for years, then we barge in and ask him to plan for the impossible.

"I would like you to formulate a safety plan in case of an attack. Give your people a safe place to go. You have an advantage with the underground tunnel system you use to grow your signature midnight flowers, correct?"

"Well...yes, those tunnels are stone and solid, but I don't see how herding everyone down there will protect us."

"The general and his army use fire and blades to burn and cut down villages like yours," I say, trying to stress the importance of his cooperation. "If you suspect danger, you can save your people by telling them to calmly escape to the tunnels. Seal them. And I will come for the heads of any who've harmed your village."

Trince studies me, sweat popping on his brow before he finally nods. "I'll get started on this right away."

I blow out a breath as I stand up. "Thank you," I say, a little of the tension relaxing in my muscles. The male wears his anxiety as clearly as his badge, but I can't really blame him. Hearing from the queen that they might be in danger would rattle me as well.

"We'll continue our efforts to stop the general's plans," I say. "Hopefully, the plan will never need to be put into practice."

"Indeed," Trince says, following us out of the building.

Blaize and Varian both visibly relax when they see me, and I do, too. Crane's brow furrows as he studies Trince, River doing much the same.

"You're not leaving already, are you, your majesty?" Trince asks when we collectively head down the main street.

I pause. "We need to get back—"

"Please," Trince interrupts me. "Please, stay until dawn. It would honor us to host our queen and her assassins."

"We really shouldn't," I say, but he bows again.

"Please," he says for the third time, an urgency in his tone. "You've done us an invaluable service, warning us about the threat. Let us repay the favor. I'll have a feast prepared fit for a queen. Surely you can spare *one* night to dine with those who support you?" His voice is raised now, proud and pleading, and other members of the village have stopped with hopeful eyes on me.

I swallow hard, the loyalty and honor gripping my throat. How can I say no to my people? How can I show up merely to warn them of impending doom and then leave? The least I can do is stay and listen and learn more about them, for the small amount of time we have.

"All right," I say, and Crane snaps his head toward me. "We will stay the evening, but we leave at daybreak."

Trince claps, a smile stretching almost too wide across his face. "We will prepare!" He spins around, hurrying to the group of onlookers who all immediately start rushing about as he delegates orders.

Crane's hand is on my elbow, tugging me around the side of the building until it's just me and him, with River, Varian, and Blaize lingering a few feet away.

"We can't stay here," he whispers.

I jerk out of his touch. "Why? We have time. It's the least I can do for these people who support me—"

"What if they don't, Ges?" he asks.

"What do you mean?"

"What if they don't support you? What if the general has already gotten to them? You saw how strange Trince was acting. You said yourself, the Slate Lands aren't far away. What if the general stopped here first and—"

"And left it intact?" I shake my head. "Stars, you will do anything to fight with me, won't you?" Pain ebbs like an icy spiderweb inside me. I'm so...heavy. This thing between us has taken every colorful and blooming feeling I had for Crane and smashed it.

"If they bowed to him, then he would leave it. I know the general—"

"So do I," I say, hatred in my tone. "I know his malice, his sick spirit. I felt it, endured it, every single night and day and..." My voice catches, tears threatening the backs of my eyes as my chest tightens.

Not here. Not now. I can't lose myself, can't panic.

I'm here, safe. Not in the dungeon. Not chained to the wall.

"Ges, please," he begs. "I know we haven't...found our way back to each other. I know that's my fault. But you have to trust me. Something about this place isn't—"

"Trust you?" I release a dark laugh. "Trust the male who left me to die every night for weeks?" I shake my head. "Trust is earned," I say, my eyes casting a glance where River and Varian and Blaize watch with careful gazes.

Each of them has earned my trust in ways Crane hasn't, and I'm just...done.

"We need to leave," Crane says, a broken expression covering his usual sharp-as-glass one.

"If you are so against every star's damned decision I make, then *you* are free to go," I snap. "I release you from whatever obligations being one of the queen's elite assassins holds you to. Do what you will."

He stumbles back a step, and the pain in his eyes lashes at my heart. A blink and it's replaced with anger as he straightens. "You want me to go, Ges?" he asks, stepping closer, hands balled into fists. "*Say* it then. Tell me to go and I will."

My entire body shakes as the battle inside me shreds my

soul. I can't keep this up with him, this twisted bond between us that does nothing but hurt and rip and cut. I can't heal if he continues to wound me at every turn.

Despite that, I want him here with me. In a way I can't understand, I need him.

But I can't need someone who does nothing but ruin me.

"Yes," I whisper, tears rolling down my cheeks. The color drains from Crane's face. "Leave, Crane. *Go*."

He shakes his head, and I swear there are tears in his eyes before he turns his back on me and sprints out of sight.

He's gone.

Just like that. With a few simple words, Crane has left my side, left me one assassin down, and a whole heap of heartbreak all over again.

And I let myself *feel* it, all of it. Everything I've held at bay with him. I open that locked box with his name carved across the top and let it spill into me. It's overwhelming and sharp, acidic in its nature. Consuming and searing and all the things I thought I wanted and needed, all the things I thought I loved about him. But there's only so many times I can stand in the center of his fire before he turns me to ash.

And I can't burn right now.

Too much is at stake. Too many people need me.

Just not the one I wanted to need me.

I swipe at the tears as I come around the side of the building, waving off Varian and River, calling *I need a minute* over my shoulder as I do my best to navigate my way through the town. It doesn't matter where I go or how far I walk, I can't outrun the hollow feeling inside me that's spreading like the first winter frost over fall leaves.

Crane left, and I'm...

Empty.

11

GESSI

I manage to distract myself with Trince's feast, listening to their village's songs while nibbling on delicacies they've provided. It's a magical sort of midnight feast, the moon high in the sky, the stars glittering like diamonds strewn across an inky blanket.

It should be enough to shake me out of the spiral I'm in, but it's not, and after I've devoted as much of my time and heart as I can to the people of the village, I make a quick escape to the beach. I've always been able to feel Crane when he's close by, but the hollowness has only gotten worse overtaking any sense of him, and I can't tell if I'm more angered or pained by that notion.

I mean, the initial shock of him actually leaving has passed, so shouldn't that buy me some kind of peace? Why am I pining for a male who has given me nothing but grief recently?

Because you know him.

I dig my bare feet into the sand, settling on a spot near a dark cove as I listen to the waves.

I used to know Crane. I used to know my friend who

would go out of his way to make me laugh when we were younglings. I used to know the male who grew up into a hardened assassin but somehow still made time to check on me, to bring me random treats from his travels. He only brought them for me, not Cari or Varian—who were his friends too—just me. I used to feel safe with his hawklike eyes watching me, watching over me...

But now? I have no idea where my friend went, and the male who just left our mission? Left me? He's someone I don't even recognize.

You swore you'd let him tell you the truth. That damn inner voice is relentless—that hollow piece of my soul that keeps crying out for him.

I would've let him tell me his side of the story. I would've let him speak his truth if he'd spared me *any* words that weren't edged in anger.

He left, and I told him to go, so maybe that makes us two sides of the same twisted and scarred coin. Maybe I'll never lose this feeling for him—the need that crashes in that hollow space inside me, but there is absolutely nothing I can do about it now.

The sand is soft and cool against my bare feet as I bring my knees up to my chest and breathe in the ocean. I don't even mind that my gown is getting covered in sand, I simply relish the beautifulness of my queendom—the midnight ocean, the glittering stars offering me the energy I need to continue on this journey, the citrusy smells from the orchard near me, the people who sang and cooked in my honor earlier. There is too much to be grateful for to sit here and dwell over Crane.

And despite knowing that in my bones, I remain seated.

"Are you going to sleep out here, love?" Varian's voice startles me so much that I jump. "Because I can fetch a blanket." He grins at me as he steps in front of me, and I glance over my shoulder, near the darkened coves.

"Have you been lingering there long?" I ask, knowing there would be no more advantageous hiding place for him to sneak up on me like that.

He raises his thumb and forefinger, the space between them minimal as he takes a seat next to me.

I move to smack his chest for spying on me, but he's so much faster, shifting his right hand into that obsidian beast of his, entrapping my hand completely. I tug and tug, but it's no use.

"You know better than that," he says as he hauls me toward him. I land against his chest and he uses his free hand to shift me onto his lap. "That's better, isn't it?" he asks, freeing my hand and shifting back into his normal form.

I relax in his arms, sighing from the contact as I swipe my fingers over my necklace.

"Why haven't you called her?" Varian asks, our faces so close our lips almost brush.

"Do you think I should?" I ask instead of answering.

He brushes some of my hair from my face. "Don't dodge my question. It's not about what I think. I want to know why *you* haven't."

I shake my head, wondering how I ever missed that this male was my mate. My true bonded mate. He's always seen to the heart of me, but he buried his passion and perceptiveness beneath sarcasm and snark. Always trying to keep me away from the monster he believes he is.

"Reasons," I say, shrugging.

He cocks a brow at me. "Well, that explains everything." He cracks a smile, and I laugh, the sensation like a balm over the hollowness that's made me cold inside.

"I will call her," I say. "If I need her." Varian studies me, eyes open and content, listening. "I want to prove myself to her. I want to make her proud, make her feel good about her decision to hand over her queendom to me."

Lines form between Varian's brows and the hand on the small of my back flexes. "You know as well as I do, Cari doesn't do anything she doesn't want to. You also know that out of everyone in all the realms, you're her favorite, and that includes her mates. You could never disappoint her."

I nod, knowing he's right, but it doesn't stop the need to do right by her choices either.

"Do you want to talk about...our other friend?" His hand traces the line of my spine, up and down over the fabric of my gown like he's soothing a wounded animal.

I swallow the emotions climbing up my throat and shake my head. "Not now," I say, leaning my forehead against his. "I can't wrap my head around what's happened to him, what's happened to us."

Varian nods against me. "When you need me," he says. "I'll be there to listen. I know you both. I want the *best* for you both."

I clench my eyes shut, knowing if anyone can understand the shit going on with Crane, it's Varian. "I don't want to talk about him right now," I say again.

"That's fair, love," he says. "What do you want, then?"

Awareness stretches inside me, blasting everything cold away with heat. "I want...for just a little while...to escape." I open my eyes, shifting on Varian's lap until one knee is on either side of him and we're chest to chest.

He smooths his hands down my back and over my hips, his touch warm and languid.

"I can help you with that," he says, slanting his lips over mine.

This kiss empties my mind until there is nothing but his

lips on mine, his tongue teasing me in torturous laps, his arms encasing me as he holds me against him. I rock against him, my gown spilling out all around us as I chase the pressure I need.

"Where can we go?" I ask between frantic kisses.

Varian leans back slightly. "River got you and him a room in the village," he says. "Blaize and I were supposed to stay on my ship..."

Lava pours into my veins.

"What if I don't want you to sleep on your ship?"

Varian's grip on me tightens, and I sigh at the way it makes my body tingle. "What are you saying, love?" He nips at my bottom lip. "You think pretty boy needs the company?" he teases. "Nah," he says, kissing his way across my jaw, stopping to tease the flesh beneath it. "You love the idea of us together, don't you?" He moves slightly beneath me, slipping one hand beneath the folds of my gown, until he's reached the apex of my thighs. He stills for a moment, rubbing the wet lace there. "Fuck, Ges, you're soaked," he says against my neck.

I move against his hand, trembling from his too-light touches.

Varian teases me in light circles, using the lace as friction on my oversensitive flesh. I ache for more, my skin practically on fire—

He withdraws his hand at the same time he plants a deliciously sharp bite on my neck. He moves so quickly I barely have time to register that he's cradling me against his chest, walking up the beach until he reaches the main street, and then a little rose-colored lodge where River must be staying.

Anticipation flares in my core, the sensation overtaking any other thought I may have had. And before I can even imagine what's about to happen, Varian is kicking open a door and slamming it closed behind us.

River leaps off the bed, wearing nothing but his under-garments, the tight black fabric exposing his muscular thighs and those lickable V-lines. For a few suspended moments, we simply stare at each other, unsure of what to say or do. These two are my mates, yes, but that doesn't mean they *have* to share me at the same time.

River tilts his head, eying me wrapped in Varian's arms, then Varian. "Is that for me?" he asks, and Varian huffs a laugh.

"For both of us," he says, and River's eyebrows raise.

I wiggle out of Varian's arms, crossing the room to River. I trail my fingers up his abs, over his chest, shocked there isn't a visible spark of electricity crackling off of me with how electrified I feel. Every touch is heightened, every need is almost unbearable. Having both my mates right here, within reach like this...it's intoxicating.

River leans down, crushing his mouth against mine in a claiming kiss that has me gasping as he wraps his arms around me. I bend to his body, his touch, as he steals my breath with expert flicks of his tongue.

In the background, I hear clothes hitting the floor and it's just enough to make both River and me break apart to look.

And stars damn me, Varian is there, crossing the room with pure confidence as he steps up behind me. But he's not looking at me, he's looking at River, and there is some serious electricity happening there too.

It makes my heart race, a delightful curiosity rising inside me.

I kiss River again, then turn my head and kiss Varian, whimpering slightly at the way they taste—wholly different and yet somehow each is perfectly made for me. I slide one hand down Varian's chest, the other down River's, until I've plunged beneath their undergarments and I'm gripping each of them.

I break our kiss, stroking their hard cocks, relishing the way they fill my hands, and move back just an inch, my gaze darting between the two of them.

"Closer," I beg, urging them together. They step closer, so close their chests nearly touch, and an ache wrenches deep in my core.

They're locked in a battle of gazes now, as if they're waiting for the other to break first. Weeks of banter and teasing have led to this moment, not to mention our bonds which are flaring to life in a braided sort of light in my soul.

My mates.

My assassins.

Mine.

Varian breaks, reaching up to grip the back of River's neck so furiously I think they may fight, but in a blink, his mouth is on River's.

It's the sexiest thing I've ever seen. The passion between my two mates, the *need*. Varian is rougher with River than he's ever been with me, and River is holding nothing back, giving Varian everything he takes in return.

I pump them harder, faster, my body tingling as I watch them.

River's hand slides down Varian's chest while they kiss, and I whimper when he trails it all the way down, over my hand, and beneath my gown, slipping it between my thighs.

"Sun damn me," he says, breaking Varian's kiss as his molten eyes find mine. "You're drenched, my queen."

Varian tightens his grip on the back of River's hair. "She enjoys watching us," he says. "Don't you, love?"

I nod, breathless, as River's fingers shift the lace to the side and slide inside me. "River," I breathe his name, trembling around his touch.

"You have to feel this," River says to Varian, who smirks and slides his hand beneath my gown too.

And then they're both touching me and I swear my knees are going to buckle. Each touch is unique, a signature to them, and I can barely breathe from wanting them both so badly.

Varian slides his finger inside me too, and I gasp at the way they both fill me as they work together to drive me mad.

River kisses down my neck while Varian teases my breasts over my gown with his free hand, and then he's tugging on the fabric, as if he's about to rip it off—

"Wait," I gasp, and the two of them freeze. "Wait," I say again, my body vehemently disagreeing with my mind for stopping this.

They each withdraw from me, giving me a few steps of space.

Each of them understands my hesitance.

Each of them is prepared to support me in whatever I ask for.

I knew without a doubt that if I asked them to stop, to give me the room, to give me time, they would.

And it's that knowledge, that absolute unflinching love between me and my mates, that has me taking a deep breath as I reach for the sleeves of my gown.

My fingers tremble as I slowly shed all the fabric covering me, letting it pool at my feet before I step out of it, baring myself to them completely.

Both of them visibly swallow, something that would be comical if I hadn't just exposed myself in the way I have.

It takes all of my willpower to not cover my stomach, to not dive under the blankets on the bed and hide myself.

"Ges," Varian says, and there is a murderous tone in his voice. "His pain will know no bounds," he says, stepping toward me, eyes on my scars.

"Slowly," River says, dropping to his knees before me. "We'll kill him slowly."

Talking about murder definitely isn't what I want to be doing right now, but I can't help the warmth that spreads out from my chest at the way they're reacting.

Not in disgust.

Not in fear or pity.

Nothing but promises to ruin the person who did this to me. The people who did this to me.

Varian's fingers trace one of the scars, and I gasp at the sensation. I can't take my eyes off his face, gauging his reaction, still searching for the repulsion that isn't there. There is nothing but need and want and love from my mate—

River's lips kiss a scar on the other side, drawing my attention to where he's on his knees, worshiping each scar like he's done with every other part of my body.

"You're beautiful," Varian says, his hand roaming over my stomach, over the hundreds of marks that were left on my body.

"So damn powerful," River says, continuing with his kissing. "To have survived this and come out stronger."

Tears well in my eyes, my heart expanding so much it hurts. "I love you," I say, and they both look at me. "Both. I love you both."

"I love you, my queen," River says, rising to his feet.

Varian grins at me. "I've loved you longer than him."

I laugh, the jab doing everything to break the tension as River rolls his eyes.

"Not everything is a competition," River says.

"If it was, I'd win," Varian fires back.

"I'm standing here completely naked before you both, and you're content to bicker with each other?" I tease, and they both turn their heated looks on me.

"Oh, that's a smart mouth you have on you," Varian says, turning his full attention to me. Chills burst along my skin at the predatory look in his eyes. "Take her to the bed, River," Varian demands, and to my utter shock, River obeys, scooping me up and laying me down on the bed in one smooth motion.

I scoot back, marveling at the sight of the two males staring me down as they stand at the foot of the bed, both sliding out of their undergarments until they're completely bare to me, cocks springing forth and all.

"You want to fight for who makes our mate come first?" Varian asks, cocking a brow at River, his face rippling just enough to tease the beast beneath his skin.

River laughs, then wets his lips. "I can be patient."

Varian smirks, wrapping his hands around my ankles and drawing me down the bed in one fast motion. My heart pounds harder in my chest as Varian kneels, his face still showing the remnants of shifting. I'm not afraid of him in any form, but there is something forbidden about seeing this side of him in this way, and it makes my body tremble.

He grins then and I see it, that tongue of his, the elongated tongue of his shifted form, and I gasp.

"You ready for this, love?" he asks, his voice slightly garbled and grainy because of the partial shift.

I nod, breathless as he dips his head between my thighs and trails that long tongue right up the center of me.

"Varian!" My hips come off the bed as he slides his tongue inside me, thrusting in and out in teasing strokes that have me writhing against him. He slips his powerful hands beneath my ass, gripping it firmly to hold me in place while he devours me.

Varian swirls his tongue around my clit before plunging it inside me again, the shifted length sliding in and out, winding me up into tight knots of need. Stars, he's amazing, an expert, as if he's been present for every time I've ever explored myself and found my favorite places to touch and tease. And somehow, he's better at it, pushing me toward that sweet, sharp edge of release that I've been teetering on since he found me on the beach.

"Fuck, that's so hot," River says, his voice closer than moments before. He's come around to the side of the bed, looking down my body to where Varian is feasting on me, and watching him watch Varian sends another gallon of lava through my veins.

River leans over me, blowing on my nipples until they're pert, and I whimper at the tease. He slides his hand over my body, cupping my breast as he rolls my nipple between his fingers, before setting his mouth on the other. I gasp, the dual sensations of having Varian's tongue between my thighs and River's on my breasts is consuming.

I grip River's hair, needing something to hold on to while both of them play and touch and tease until I'm breathless and tight all over. My thighs clench around Varian's head, and he groans, upping the pace of his feasting, flatting that tongue of his to give me all the pressure I need—

"Varian!" I cry out his name as my orgasm tears through me, and before I can say another word, River is covering my mouth with his, as if he wants to drink in my moans.

My head is spinning as River kisses me, still exploring

and teasing my breasts, before we feel a shift of weight on the bed.

We break our kiss, and Varian is there on his knees, smirking down at me with nothing but pure satisfaction on his face as he licks his lips.

"Fucking delicious, love," he says, then turns his attention to River. In a move almost too fast to follow, he grabs River's shoulder, flipping him to his back as Varian hovers an inch above his face. "Want a taste?" he asks, and I swear I go wholly liquid again at the sight of the two of them. These glorious, gorgeous males—my *mates*—one suspended above the other, their massive thighs touching, their cocks hard and pressed against each other.

"Yes," River says, and Varian slants his mouth over his. I watch as his tongue parts his lips and relish the groan that rumbles through River's chest. "I can taste her on your tongue," he sighs between Varian's lips, reaching up to grip Varian's neck, jerking him harder against him.

I roll to my side, one hand roaming over my own skin because I just can't help myself. Watching them makes me ache, makes all the nerves in my body come alive in a way I never knew possible.

Varian is relentless and powerful as he claims River's mouth, the sight sending bolts of lightning throughout my body. I'm content to watch this for the rest of forever when Varian pulls back, planting a bite on River's chest that makes him hiss, before Varian draws back and reaches for me.

I go to him instantly, whimpering as he kisses me, the taste of all three of us on his tongue. "Why don't you sit that sweet pussy on River's cock?" Varian says, motioning to where River is still laying on his back.

I crawl past Varian, situating myself on top of River. I

grip his cock, stroking it through my heat, teasing us both before I sink atop it.

"Fuck," River groans, hips thrusting upward enough to make me gasp. "You're so hot, so wet."

"You're welcome," Varian says from behind me, and I can't help but smile. Neither can River. "Ride him," Varian says, and I rock atop River, my thighs trembling as I move up and down on his hard cock, relishing the way he fills me.

River grips my hips, eyes molten dark as he watches me ride him.

Varian slides his hand up my back, settling in right behind me. The heat from both of them has me aching, urging me to go faster, harder, but Varian reaches around me, stilling me with a powerful arm.

He pushes on my back, laying me flat against River's chest, and I turn to glance over my shoulder at him. He smirks at me, looking down at my exposed ass before raising his hand and spitting on it, rubbing his wet fingers over my tight hole, drenching it before he slides a finger in.

"Stars," I gasp, my body like liquid heat as he slides that finger in and out of me a few more times before pulling out. He grips my hip and lines his cock up.

"Tell me to stop, love," Varian says. "And I will." He hesitates, holding me in exquisite anticipation.

I can't breathe.

"Don't stop," I beg. "Please. Don't. Stop."

Varian slides in an inch, then another, the fit so damn tight.

My heart is racing as he fills me from behind, River filling me from beneath.

"Fuck, look at you," Varian says, drawing me out of the spiral of sensation my mind is whipping through. "Look how good you take both our cocks." He grips my hips now, slowly thrusting into me from behind, which causes me to rock against River. "Doesn't she take our cocks so fucking well, Riv?"

"Fuck right she does," River says, his lips finding mine. "Perfection."

I moan, my entire body alive with sensation, with need. I move on River while Varian thrusts into me from behind, the three of us finding our rhythm in a matter of seconds. Soon, I'm reaching back, gripping Varian's thigh with one hand, urging him to fuck me harder while I grip River's hand with the other.

"Ges," Varian groans as I up our pace, hungry with need, desperate to clash and meld on every single level possible. "*Fuck.*"

River kisses my neck and groans every time I sink atop him, fueling my relentless need, while Varian drives home over and over again.

Stars, everything inside me is coiling, braiding together so tightly I know I'll snap soon. Our bonds are bright strings of light between us, touching and twining until I can't tell where one ends and the other begins.

I can feel them both inside me, pumping and thrusting, and I know they can feel each other, and somehow that is the most intimate and intoxicating thing I've ever felt before. My mates, my assassins, together in every way we can be, and I fucking love it.

My body is made for them, the way we fit together a recipe for ultimate pleasure. My breathing is quick, my skin slick with sweat as we writhe against each other, an unmatched unit of love and passion and need.

I raise up as much as I can, needing more control as Varian drives into me, River now thrusting up from beneath me, the two of them downright primal in their claiming.

River's hands are on my hips, holding me captive while the two of them have their way with me, and I can't help but run my hands over my breasts, relishing the sensation as I push back against them both, claiming them as much as they're claiming me.

And it pushes me right over the edge, the sensation of them both filling me, claiming me, devouring me. It shoves me into orbit as I clench around them both, a thousand sparks igniting through me as I come.

"*Ges*," Varian groans. "Fuck, River, can you feel that?"

"Yes," River says, his grip on my hips tightening. "I feel you both," he groans as I continue to flutter and clench around them. "Feels so fucking good."

Varian tangles a hand in my hair, gently gripping it by the roots as he drives into me faster than before. River matches his pace, sending one orgasm spiraling right into another until they both come, their groans sending shivers of delight across my skin.

After taking a few moments to catch our breath, both River and Varian gently slide out of me, and hurry to clean me up. Their care is attentive and endearing, and they work together as if we've done this a thousand times before—one ensuring I drink plenty of water while the other slides comfortable pajamas over my happily weakened body.

When they're both content I've been properly taken care of, they settle on either side of me in the bed, enveloping me in the best, most comforting cocoon of safety and devotion I've ever felt before.

And as our breathing evens out, sleep calling to all three of us, I wonder how in the stars I got so damn lucky.

12

GESSI

"We need to move," Blaize's voice rips me from a deep sleep.

I jolt upright in bed, my brain taking a few seconds to remember exactly where I'm at.

The orchard village, in a lodge, with Varian and River on either side of me.

I grip the sheet to cover my body as I focus on Blaize. He's in full battle leathers, armed to the teeth with knives and his signature blaster, his silver arm winking in the low light flickering in the room.

"What's happened?" I ask as Varian and River switch into assassin mode, leaping out of bed in search of their clothes.

Blaize cringes, spinning around. "That's a whole lot of dick before breakfast," he says, shaking his head.

"If you're jealous, join us next time," Varian teases while slipping into his fighting leathers.

Heat rushes over my body at the thought, but it's quickly whisked away by the rigid way Blaize is standing, not to mention him barging into this room without a second thought. I hurry off the bed, digging through my pack for my own leathers, and sliding into them so Blaize can't see the scars. They settle around me like a warm glove, the material supple yet strong, hugging my curves as my power crackles to life in my veins.

"What's happening?" River asks, his signature red and black leather suit fitted to his body, all manner of gadgets strapped to his belt.

Blaize turns back around, eyes darting between each of us.

"Trince's scouts spotted two of the general's guards heading this way. They're about fifteen minutes out."

My blood runs cold. "Any sign of the general?"

"How do they know they're the general's guards?" Varian asks at the same time.

"No sign of the general," Blaize answers me first. "The scouts say they've seen the standard uniform for the royal guards before."

I bite my lip. I'd ordered all of my royal guards' uniforms to be changed the second I came into power. I didn't want them bearing the previous king's or the general's moniker on their chests anymore. Instead, they now wore leather as black as the ocean, with a simple night-blooming flower branding their right arms to show they work with me.

Unless, of course, you were in my elite assassin guard— like Varian, River, Blaize, and Crane—they wore whatever they chose and damn anyone who tries to tell them differently. But my Shattered Isle assassins under Lance's command? They were proud to shed the general's and king Jerrick's marks and replace them with mine. It had been a testament to their support of their new queen, and it had touched me deeply.

Whoever is approaching the orchard village now must

still wear the old uniforms for the scouts to have spotted them.

"Why would only two be heading this way?" I ask, shoving my feet into my boots. If the general had heard of my arrival here, wouldn't he come with his entire army?

"Let's go ask them," Varian says, his eyes lighting up like a youngling on winter solstice.

"I agree," Blaize says, nodding.

"I'm in," River adds, opening the door and waving his arm toward Varian and Blaize.

"I'm coming too," I say, and I meet each other their eyes, daring any of them to stop me. To convince me that the queen of the Shattered Isle shouldn't put herself at risk like that. Crane most certainly would've.

"Of course you are," Blaize says, stepping toward me as Varian and River file out the door. "You have as much stake in this as any of us."

Those words, such simple, supportive words, have my heart expanding for the cool, icy All Plane warrior—

No. He's a Shattered Isle elite assassin. *My* Shattered Isle elite assassin, and I feel ten times more powerful as I head out the door with him on my heels. Because my team, my support system, my mates...they have my back in a way that makes me feel fearless as I march toward the unknown.

We make our way as quietly as possible through the main town. The little village is just now waking up as night takes over the day. The scouts are on hold, prepared to launch the safety measures Trince worked on the previous night if we give the signal. But if there are only two guards, they really won't pose a threat. Which somehow worries me more than if the general and his entire army were bearing down on us.

Why two?

It doesn't make sense. Unless they truly have no clue we're here, and it's merely a coincidence that they're heading this way. Maybe they're here to cause trouble, prey on the innocent village and pillage their supplies.

Not tonight, not while I'm here.

We slip out of the main town, passing the lush orchards as we prepare to meet the guards before they get close enough to the village to do any damage. Thank the stars the scouts caught sight of them early to give us this advantage.

The night sky is fully broken over the purple sunset by the time we reach the exteriors of the village. I follow River, ducking behind the cover of a jutting rock on the right side of the beach while Varian and Blaize take cover on the left. I slow my breathing, my power twisting like growing vines in my blood as we wait.

Their footsteps are clunky even in the sand as they approach—males, two of them, just as the scouts said. They're laughing at something as they walk right past us, seemingly nonchalant, as if they were on a perimeter patrol of a controlled area.

River raises his fingers at me, counting down…

Three, two, one—

He taps a button on his custom suit and disappears, and my body jolts at the sight. I'm still not used to his technology, his inventions and gadgets, and I don't know if I will ever be. Which is strange, since Varian shifting into a stretchable, nearly indestructible monster does nothing to jar me.

In seconds, I'm whirling around the rock, curling my fingers as I call to the sand around the guards' boots. I clench my fists, and the two guards halt. They grunt as they try to pull their legs from the sand, but they're immobilized.

Their weapons disappear seconds later, floating through

the air as if someone here has the telekinetic abilities like the general. Ice chills my blood, my power slipping just a fraction at the idea of him being here, and I can't see him.

River. It's River. He's disarming them. Just because I can't see him doesn't mean he isn't there.

I repeat the words until I feel solid and the memories of the general's torture stop sending chills over my skin.

"What are you doing here?" I ask, keeping my chin held high as I wave my fingers at them again, creating ropes from the sand and securing their arms to the sides.

They look identical in their old guard uniforms, both wearing looks of disgust and prideful stubbornness as I walk around the two of them.

River returns to his normal size right next to me. The guards jolt in surprise, straining against their bonds.

I lean down, recognizing the two from the palace. They weren't the general's favorites, but held their own in the lower ranks of the previous assassin guard. "I'll ask you again," I say, my voice seething. "What are you doing here?"

Something cold and wet hits my face. I jerk back, swiping at the spit one of the guards launched at me.

River moves with lightning quickness, slapping something on the spitter's neck before pressing a button on a tiny control in his hand. The spitter goes stark stiff as volts of electricity crackle over his skin. He grinds his teeth, groaning against the pain as he drools on himself.

"That's one," River says, pushing the control in his hand again. The spitter sighs, his body still twitching. "You don't get another."

"Please don't make me ask again," I say, twirling my fingers before them and tightening the sand hard enough to hear their bones pop.

"The queen asked you a question," Varian's garbled voice

sounds from the darkness next to us seconds before he stalks into sight before the guards.

Stars, he's a sight to behold when he's fully shifted. A sleek, powerful obsidian exterior ripples over tons of corded muscle. He's three times as tall as his normal form, his razor-sharp teeth stretching into a terrifying smile, that delightful, elongated tongue flicking out enough to make the guards jump in their bonds. Varian's eyes are wholly changed too—nothing but oversized white orbs, the eyes of death personified as he stares them down.

"Look," Blaize says, coming to join our group, blaster in hand. "They're trembling."

"I have that effect," Varian says in that rough, beast-like voice, before glancing over his shoulder and winking one of those pure white eyes at me.

I shake my head, but can't really hold back my grin. Varian is fearless, with good reason, and finds humor in everything. That's probably why he and River get along so well. They both think they're the funniest one in the room.

Varian stretches an obsidian arm toward the spitter, curling it around his neck like the sand ropes I've made. He moves, reaching his other hand toward the opposite guard—

"We heard you were here!" the guard yells, his entire body shaking at the sight of Varian. "We heard you were here," he repeats, panic coating his eyes.

Varian pauses, and he doesn't need to turn around to show he's waiting for me to continue.

"How?" I ask.

"A contact," the trembling guard says, flinching as Varian continues to stretch that hand toward him.

"And what are your orders?" I ask. "Where are you stationed?" He couldn't be with the general's main army because they were last spotted leaving the northern edge of the Slate Lands. They wouldn't have been able to make it back here that fast.

"A village over," he stutters, and the spitter is glaring at him, but he can't speak thanks to Varian's arm around his throat. "The herbalists," he continues. "We've taken possession."

"How many of you are there?" I ask, my heart clenching at the idea of the village being under their control.

"Twenty."

Twenty we can handle, if he's being truthful, which I highly doubt. I'll have to call Lance to send another party of assassins this way to ensure we give the herbalists their village back.

"You didn't answer my first question," I say, sliding my hands along Varian's arm—his shifted form feeling like silk-covered iron. He loosens his grip on the spitter's neck. No need to kill them when we're actively trying to get information out of them.

The terrified guard dips his head so low I can't see his eyes.

Varian pulls his arm back, and the spitter coughs, sucking in air, and then he *laughs*.

It's unnerving and icy and emotionless, and his eyes meet mine. They're like two pools of oil, nothing but malice settling there.

Frosty spiders skitter over my skin at the look, the laugh, and—

A crashing boom shakes the earth.

And then the screams start.

13

GESSI

"**D**istract you!" the spitter yells over the roars of the explosion, over the agonized screams piercing the night sky.

I whirl around, seeing the flames even from this distance.

"The village," I gasp, my power slipping in my veins like sand through my fingers.

One second. That's all it takes.

Spitter slams into me from behind, the hit like a hammer to the chest as we smack into the sand. His weight is at least twice mine, suffocating and thick as he jerks me onto my back and bangs his fist into my jaw.

Stars burst behind my eyes, a metallic tang filling my mouth as blood pools there.

Spitter is grinning manically as he cocks his fist back, and I reach for my power through the stun of his hit—

A loud boom shakes the air and his eyes go wide before he topples off of me.

Blaize is there, blaster aimed at where Spitter had just been. I suck in a sharp breath, my mind returning to my body as I wipe at the green blood on the corner of my mouth.

"Get up," Blaize demands, the authority in his voice unmatched, primal. It *does* things to my body—gilds it with strength, fills my muscles, and clears my head as I leap to my feet.

I rise just in time to see the other guard jab a small knife into Varian's side. I jolt, gasping as I take two steps toward my mate—

Only to watch him rip the guard's head clean from his body with his powerful, shifted hands.

I freeze, pursing my lips as he sends the two different pieces of the body soaring in opposite directions.

"He had that coming," Varian growls, and the rage in my heart at the sight of my mate being harmed has me agreeing wholeheartedly.

"Move," Blaize orders, and my entire being shifts at the command. I'm moving toward the village, racing at Blaize's side as River disappears and Varian leaps enormous bounds ahead of us. "Show off!" Blaize grumbles as we're forced to hoof it.

Blaize is fast though, his speed pushing me to my limits as I hurry to keep pace with him. We make it to the village in record time and I skid to a halt on the main street.

It's burning. The beautiful jewel-colored buildings are covered in flames and there are at least two dozen of the general's guards stomping through the carnage, stabbing and shooting and killing at random.

Sorrow climbs up my throat, such devastation at the sight of so much innocent blood being shed that it threatens to choke me.

A guard hurtles our direction, a glimmering blade aimed just for me as he leaps—

Blaize catches him by his throat with that silver arm of his, stopping the attacker dead in his tracks. A crack sounds and Blaize drops the guard in a heap on the ground.

I gape at him, at that beautifully tattooed arm, and arch a brow.

He shrugs. "Just because I don't show off doesn't mean I don't have my own talents," he says, then jerks his head toward the raging battle. "You going to stand here and let this happen? Queen?"

Fire ignites in me, stronger and fiercer than the flames blazing all around us. "No," I say, determined, as we move in unison toward the carnage.

Another guard has a group of females huddled against one of the buildings that hasn't caught fire yet, his two glimmering swords poised to cut them all down.

The power in my veins mounts as I create sharp, spindly vines and send them soaring for him. They make a home around his neck, squeezing so hard his eyes bleed. His swords clatter to the ground just before he does, and the females hurry in the opposite direction, casting looks of gratitude over their shoulders.

They're heading for the tunnels, I notice. Most of the terrified villagers flee that direction, the ones who've escaped the flames and guards, anyway. Good. Trince's safety plan is working.

New screams are adding to the surrounding chaos, but these are more guttural. I whirl toward the sound to see Varian leaping and chomping and ripping. My beast, my monster in the night, tearing through the guards as if they were paper dolls. The fleeing villagers note my shifted mate, but don't cower in fear, instead doing their best to stay out of his way as he buys them time. Six. Varian shreds *six* of them in a matter of heartbeats.

Another four fall on the other side of main street, their attacker invisible. River.

Shots crack through the air as Blaize fires his blaster, sending another five to their deaths.

I swear I see arrows flying, but I know it has to be my imagination since Crane isn't here.

On and on the battle goes, but that fire...*it's* doing the most damage. Spreading like a disease content to eradicate this town. Five buildings have already succumbed to it, and it's working its way down the main road, hungry for more.

Some brave souls are dumping buckets of water on it, trying to tame the wild flames, but it barely makes a dent.

"Move!" I yell as I race toward the bulk of the flames. "Move to the tunnels. Now!" I command at those trying to put out the fire. They drop their buckets, abandoning what is likely their livelihoods or homes as they race away.

I raise my arms, closing my eyes as I call on all the power I have.

This is going to hurt.

My powers thrash and strain as I beckon the beach to me, the soft sand floating in the air as it races toward where I command. I dump tons and tons of sand on the flames, smothering the life out of them one by one.

Sweat pops on my brow. The weight of the sand, the amount I need to stop this, is a crushing weight that makes me feel like a matchstick holding up a sky-ship.

I groan, my teeth clenching as I hit building after building, the flames snuffing out until they are nothing but impressions on the backs of my eyelids. My power wanes as I release the sand, the grains spilling along the charred building walls and piling into the street, but it burns no longer.

"You said you would only take them!" Trince's voice

rings clear now that the flames have died and most of the villagers have made it to the safety of the tunnels.

I turn, finding him scrambling on the ground as a guard stalks toward him.

"You said you only wanted them! Why do this? I called you! I gave you what you wanted!" Trince raises his arms in defense, and before I can move, the guard slices through his neck without half a thought.

Crane was right. Trince had been a traitor, but that didn't mean I could damn his people for his actions. Fuck, now I can't even interrogate Trince about it.

The guard scans the area, spotting me on my knees in the middle of the main road. He stomps toward me, and I manage to haul myself to my feet. My power is nothing but wisps in my blood, but I cling to the dregs I have left.

Varian is on the roof a block away, finishing a handful of guards who had been shooting at fleeing villagers.

River is unseen but likely the cause of the guards falling behind me.

And Blaize has lost his blaster as he battles two more across the road, that silver arm flexing, the red star like a warning flare for any who approach.

I tip my chin, finding strength in my bonds. My mates are defending this village. *I* am defending it. And together, we will not let these attacks stand.

"You missed some," I say, pointing to the pristine, unburned buildings lining the other side of the road. The guard huffs, raising his sword toward me. At least this one isn't armed with a blaster. I'll take what luck I can right now, especially with my powers still trying to rebuild after I stopped the blaze.

"The only one that truly matters is right here," he grinds out the words, and I don't recognize his voice or his face. Just another of the general's pets that he kept so confined to training and vile missions.

I almost feel sorry for him.

Almost.

He charges me, sword swiping to cut me down—

It hits a wide, circular shield of solid oak, the blade sinking nearly halfway through my attempt to block him. Mustering the shield drains me, but I manage to shove him back with a kick to the stomach.

He's got so much weight on me, though, it doesn't faze him much. Stars, I need to work on my hand-to-hand training. I've grown rusty ever since Cari left. We used to train together, her insisting I learn everything she learned in case the time ever came to defend myself.

Well, I guess that time is now, because my powers are just about tapped. My eyes are heavy, my bones are heavy, everything about me feels like I'm sinking.

Too much. I used too much. I know better, but I can't really find the energy to care. The fire is out, the village is spared, and my assassins are on their way to stopping the rest of the guards. This is a win. No matter what happens here, this is a win.

"Stupid little girl playing at queen," the guard says, coming at me again. His sword hits my shield repeatedly. The force reverberates through the wood and down my arms, turning my arms to jelly. "You'll bow to me before this night is done."

Anger shakes me as I shove against him, trying like hell to fend him off, but he just keeps coming. The breath in my lungs is thin and my muscles are waning just as much as my power. But...I will not go down like this.

I didn't falter when the general had me locked in that

cell. Didn't break when his knives or Erix's claws shredded me over and over again. I will not die like this.

Calling on the last of my power, I fashion a sharp wooden blade and conceal it. The timing has to be right for this to work, so I drop my shield, showing the guard everything he wants to see. My exhaustion, my fear, my inescapable worry.

He grins. "On your knees."

"I would rather die."

"Suit yourself. What the general doesn't know won't hurt him."

Acid claws up my throat, but I tip my chin, motioning at him to come at me.

"Gessi!" Blaize roars, but he's too far away.

The guard rushes me, sword high above his head.

Just a little closer.

There.

He brings the sword down, aimed right at the soft flesh of my neck. I duck to the side at the last second, slamming my wooden dagger into his throat at the same time. His blade clips my leg as he drops it, and the searing heat slashes at my skin. I hobble out of his path just before he falls to the ground, choking on his own blood as he tries to dislodge the dagger.

He's not alive long enough to do that.

Blaize crashes to a halt at my side. "What the hell were you thinking, huh?" His voice is strained as he drops to his knees, examining the wound on my leg.

"That he needed to die," I say simply.

Blaize looks up at me and laughs, shaking his head as he stands up and scoops me into his arms.

"Ges?" Varian calls from the rooftop.

"I've got her!" Blaize shouts. "Have River help the villagers. You ensure we got them all."

Varian nods as Blaize whisks me across the street, into the nearest building. It looks like a market with rows and rows of wooden crates displaying every fruit the village is known for producing.

Blaize sets me on a long, rectangular table, likely used for a display but is thankfully empty.

"I'm fine," I say as he fusses over me.

He cocks a brow at me, hurrying around the market, grabbing supplies before rushing back to me. "It's shallow," he says, cleaning the wound on my leg.

"I told you, I'm fine."

"You didn't look fine," he says, and I huff a laugh.

"Thanks," I say, and he rolls his eyes as he wraps the tiny cut. "Is that necessary?"

"Yes," he says, his fingers lingering on my skin as he rises. His wintry eyes widen as he sees something on my stomach.

I glance down and go entirely still. I don't know if it was this most recent fight or putting out the fire, but my leathers have been ripped open, revealing some of the scars along my torso.

Blaize reaches out, grazing a trembling finger over one of my scars, the touch searing. His jaw clenches as he locks eyes with me.

"Who did this to you?"

I swallow hard.

River and Varian had seen them and worshiped me in a way that made me feel better about the scars, but Blaize...he doesn't look like he's about to comfort me. He looks like he's about to murder someone. Or several someones. It makes anticipation flood through my veins, awakening my senses in a way that clears my mind completely.

"Who did this to you, Gessi?" he asks again, and there is something about the way he says my name, all wrapped in need and desperation and anguish that has my soul shifting inside, like peeling back a layer and revealing...

Oh. My. Stars.

Blaize flinches slightly, as if he feels it too.

"It depends on which scar you're asking about," I finally say, just to break the mounting tension between us.

Blaize studies me for a moment, and my heart seems to hang on whatever he is about to say. He folds his arms over his chest, nodding toward me.

"Show me," he demands in that authoritative way of his. The same tone that sends tendrils of heat cascading over my nerves every single time he uses it.

I hesitate for only a moment before I grip the bottom of my top and peel it up and over my head. I sit up straighter, resisting the urge to cover my breasts. Blaize is my assassin, my friend, my challenger, and my...stars, he's my...

"Fuck," he growls, his eyes roaming over my exposed flesh. His arms drop to his sides as he stalks back to me, those silver fingers outstretched. He gauges my reaction as he trails one of his fingers over a scar near my hip. "This one," he says.

"The general," I answer, my breath trembling. His touch is like a brand, awakening that silvery string of light inside me, the one with his name emblazoned across it. "His favorite blade."

"And this one," he says, trailing that finger over a vertical scar going straight down my middle. I shiver under his touch, amazed at the way I'm able to stay rooted in this moment when speaking about the events that have stopped me cold for hours at a time.

"Erix," I say, almost hissing the name. The memory of the cat-like shifter makes my stomach turn. "He's a shifter, too. Used his claws." I run my fingers down the scar, the largest one surrounded by hundreds of others, turning my once smooth stomach into a textured, chaotic mess. "I thought this was the one," I continue. "The one to end it all. The general was furious with him. Had to bring in a healer." I swallow back a mouthful of acid. "The general didn't want me dead just yet, but Erix got carried away." I shake my head. "He delights in torture, that one."

Blaize moves his hands and takes a step away from me, his entire body shaking as he balls his hands into fists. His eyes meet mine, and I immediately hop off the table, ignoring the pain from the cut on my leg.

"Don't you dare!" I snap, and his lips part in shock.

"What the hell are you talking about?" he snaps right back.

I stop mere inches away from him, tilting my chin so I can hold his gaze. I point at his eyes. "You don't pity me, Blaize. You don't back away from me and start treating me like glass! Not *you*."

His eyes drop to my torso again and the rage that fuels his features is palpable. "I'm not treating you like glass," he snaps. "I stepped away because I need to break something," he continues, raising his silver arm and curling his fingers. "Need to dig these into that bastard's chest and rip out his fucking heart."

My breath quickens. "Why?"

"Why?" He glares down at me. "Do you really not know?"

Know why he'd want to rip Erix's heart out? Yes. Yes, I think I know.

I reach up, my hand trembling as I lay my palm flat over his chest. "I know," I say. "I think I've known it since the second you walked into the palace—"

Blaize moves faster than I can follow, slanting his mouth over mine. There is nothing gentle about this kiss, nothing soft. Blaize is all primal dominance, consuming strokes, and claiming laps. He tangles his fingers in my hair, tipping my head back just enough to break our kiss.

"Say it," he demands. "I want to hear you *say* it."

"Mate," I breathe the word. "Blaize, you're my mate."

His eyes gutter, his entire body shuddering against me as the bond buried deep inside us crackles to life with the acknowledgement.

"Please," I beg. "Don't change. Don't treat me like I'll break at any moment. I can't stand the thought. Not from you."

A battle rages over his features, some internal struggle I can almost feel rippling down the bond. Then, in a blink, it's gone.

He releases me and takes a step away. I swear I internally flinch at that movement.

"Take those off." He eyes my pants, and warmth floods my body.

I quickly take off my pants, careful of the wrapping he'd done on my leg. It doesn't even hurt anymore. Not now, not when this is happening. Even my powers are spiraling, building as they feed off the bond awakening and strengthening between us.

Blaize takes his time, trailing his eyes over my body, studying every curve, every patch of skin, smooth and marred. Slowly, he walks in a circle around me, the heat blazing between us enough to make me whimper. I ache for him in a way that is ancient and primal and needy. This bond, our mating bond, wants us to consummate it at any cost. Forget that we just fought a battle, forget that my other mates are tending to the aftermath of that event right this second. This goes beyond that.

He stops before me, shedding his clothes in an effortless motion. His muscles are carved, but the smooth skin over them has its own set of scars, too. We're the same in so many ways and sometime, I want him to tell me how he got his just like I told him how I got mine. But now...now isn't the time.

He knows it.

I know it.

We likely only have minutes before one of my other mates comes to find us, and while I love the idea of all three of them having their way with me, there is something pinnacle in this moment with Blaize.

I need him, and only him right now.

"Turn around," he demands, that tone making me tight with anticipation. I do as I'm told, relishing the dominance in his voice. "Walk to the table."

I do.

"Bend over it," he demands. "Hands on the edge."

Flames lick beneath my skin as I do as I'm told.

Blaize comes up behind me, sliding his hands over my back, down my ass, and between my thighs. "You're a good fucking girl, aren't you?"

Warmth glitters down my spine, and I nod.

Blaize nudges my feet farther apart before settling behind me, dipping his hard cock through what is already slick for him. I sigh at the contact, my body aching for all of him.

"Are you going to be as good taking my cock?" he asks, leaning over me, planting kisses down my back.

I arch backward, needing more of him. "Yes," I promise.

He leans up, grabbing the globes of my ass with each hand. "When we have time," he says. "I'm going to mark this ass so good, you'll forget every other mark but mine."

I tremble at that promise.

"But right now," he continues, sliding his silver arm around my thigh, teasing me from the front. "We don't have much time."

I gasp at those strong fingers, at the power in them as he strokes me, teases me. It's unlike anything I've ever felt as he slides in and out of me before rubbing circles around my clit. It's like heat and power and something supercharged I can't explain. Whatever talent he spoke of earlier with this silver arm is most certainly not confined to battle. Because *stars,* he's already worked me to the edge—

"Blaize!" I gasp as he increases his pace to speeds that can't be achieved normally, to pressures that can't be achieved normally, the combination sending me soaring right over that sharp edge until I shatter into a million pieces.

I catch my breath, limp against the table, as I turn my head to look back at him.

His smirk sends bolts of fire through the center of me. And then he raises those fingers to his lips and licks off my flavor. He moans around the taste. "I've wanted to know what you taste like since I first set eyes on you," he says.

I blow out a breath, unable to form one coherent thought after what he just did to me. I move to rise from the table, but he gently nudges me back down, the woodgrain pressing against my bare breasts with the sweetest friction.

"I didn't tell you we were done yet."

14

BLAIZE

Gessi tastes like citrus and spring water and mountain snow. She tastes like a fucking treat concocted especially for me.

Mate.

Gessi is my mate.

I suspected when Steel first ordered me to her side, but I never wanted to believe it. Never could allow myself to believe it. Things like that don't happen to me. To Steel? Absolutely. He deserves the world and more. He's good to his core. He's comprised of real life-changing, world-bettering stuff.

Me?

Mine is icy with chasms of darkness from my past that can never be filled with light. I accepted that a long time ago. I've owned it every day of my life, resigned myself to never be *whole* after everything I've gone through. Everything I've done.

But the bright green chain of light flickering to life inside me? The one that connects me to Gessi in the most ancient and primal way? It's teasing me with happiness, with joy, with hope. Things I haven't felt in a very long time.

And I'm not strong enough to deny it. If I was a better male, I'd deny the bond. Not chain Gessi to a cold warrior like me.

But this is the first thing I can't beat.

Because I want her, I need her, and I'm going to make damn sure she knows it.

"Keep your hands where they are," I command, and she shivers against me. My mate likes to be told what to do and lucky for her, I love barking out demands. We're made for each other in every way possible, and I'm more than fucking ready to see how we fit together. "You move them, I stop," I say, gliding my aching cock through her wetness. She came for me in a matter of seconds, my sweet, pliable mate. She's more than ready for me. "You understand?"

"Yes," she says, all compliant.

Fuck, just the sight of her like this, sprawled over the table, all submissive with her glorious ass pressed against my hips, has me leaking precome from my dick.

I take my time, roaming my hands over her back, noting the scars peppered there. Fury rises up inside me again, but I stow it away for later. The monsters who put these scars here will fucking suffer. No doubt about it. But now...now she needs me to treat her like I would normally.

I grip a handful of her hair, tipping her head back just enough for me to lean over her and graze my lips over the shell of her ear. "You may be the queen of the Shattered Isle," I say, nipping at her ear. "But here, in my hands? You belong to *me*."

Gessi whimpers, her entire body shivering against me. Fuck, she feels so soft and warm, so breakable beneath me.

But her power is rising, rebuilding after what she'd spent earlier, and it perks up to test my own.

"I'm yours," she whispers, and the words unravel me.

I shift behind her, sliding my cock in inch by inch until I'm seated to the hilt.

"Fuck," I groan, giving her a moment to adjust to my size. She's all heat and silk and slickness around me. I lean even farther back, pulling out and sliding in again, watching as my cock glides into her like a dream. "You look so beautiful taking my cock."

"Blaize," she sighs, gripping the edge of the table as I glide into her again.

And again.

Each time I thrust inside her, that bond between us brightens in my soul.

Each time she takes me, my heart shifts, adjusting to take her in too.

Each time we slam home, that mating bond twists and braids into something unbreakable.

I reach down, gripping her hair as I increase my pace, helpless against the need driving me. Her moans fuel my pumps, the slickness of her sweet pussy making it so fucking easy to go fast.

"You're such a good fucking girl," I say. "All slick and warm for me."

Her grip tightens on the table to the point I can hear it creak and her pussy flutters around me.

"Blaize," she moans, and the sound has my body clenching, too. "I'm going to come," she breathes the words, her body shivering as her orgasm builds.

I switch to slow, hard thrusts that leave her breathless as I edge her. I move my fingers from her hair around to her throat, gripping it as I haul her upright against me, her back pressed to my chest as I slide in and out of her.

She moans as I gently squeeze my fingers around her throat, increasing the pressure there as I continue to lengthen my thrusts. Her entire body trembles against mine, her eyes submissive and glazed as she looks up at me from behind.

Mine.

Completely and utterly mine.

Her throat in my grip, my cock buried inside her, her moans music to my ears. There is nothing between us but trust and need, and it makes everything in me narrow to that certainty.

I edge her until she reaches up and tangles her fingers in my hair, gripping the strands tight enough to sting. And just when I feel her clamp down around me, just when her cries are a combination of pleasure and desperation, I pound into her hard and fast.

Claiming her while the mating bond binds us together, weaving our two souls into something new, something powerful.

"Blaize, please," she cries, her voice a whisper from my grip on her throat. She's so slick I can feel her trickling down my thighs. "*Stars*," she groans as I shove her right over that edge I built.

And I soar right over it with her.

I see stars as I empty inside her, spilling into her with a growl.

Our breathing slows as we come down, and I lean over her, planting kisses all along her neck and back. Stroking her through the aftershocks until we're both sated.

The bliss lasts for only moments before the sounds of reality filter in through the closed doors of the market.

There aren't any more screams, but I can hear River speaking to villagers, directing them to safe spots or places for medical attention.

One look at my mate and I know.

We have to go.

We dress quickly, and I'm relieved to see she's not favoring the leg with the minor cut on it. I may have promised her I wouldn't treat her like glass, but that doesn't mean I'll stop worrying about her. I always have. She just hasn't noticed.

I gently grip her elbow when she reaches the doors to the market, looking more energized and whole than she did when we came in here. I part my lips, but the words are a jumble in my mind.

She smiles up at me, a silent promise in her eyes.

This moment may be over between us, but it's only the beginning.

And that gives me what I need to let her walk out the door, me trailing behind her, with nothing but the unknown ahead of us.

15

GESSI

It took us two entire nights to get both the orchard village and the herbalists' village straightened out. Luckily, the casualties had been low for the battle in the orchard village, and the herbalists suffered no losses. We tended to the wounded and the second Lance's teams landed to deal with any straggling traitors—those who were loyal to Trince and his determination to sell us out—my assassins and I left as swiftly as we could.

We'd arrived in the Onyx City an hour ago, and were currently waiting not-so-patiently in a stunningly pristine room made of the land's namesake. Smooth, midnight furniture fills the room, several chairs and tables scattered about in the city's political center. Crystal chandeliers cast the room in a twinkling glow that make the room look like it's made of night incarnate, only further speaking of the wealth of this place. The leader of the Onyx City—Huxton Dale—had yet to arrive. From my research, the Onyx City has always been loyal to the Shattered Isle rulers of the past, but with such a drastic change...it's hard to know for sure where their loyalties lie.

"Do you think we have something to fear here?" River asks Varian quietly as he leans against a stone pillar on the opposite side of the room, the flecks of gray contrasting with his crimson suit.

Varian paces the space before him, looking like a prowling cat strategizing his next hunt. "I think after the last village, we should tread carefully."

Pain twists my nerves, a sinking sort of sensation. Trince made a choice under dire circumstances. Who is to say I wouldn't have bent to the general if my entire people were threatened? Selling us out though...that was a blow I would not soon recover from, even if I mildly understood it.

Blaize drops into the chair next to me, folding his arms over his chest. There's a hard set to his jaw, his black hair disheveled in a way that makes him look both endearing and murderous at the same time. "They've kept us waiting too long," he says, his voice icy, but his thigh brushes mine, sending shivers soaring over my skin. "Who's to say they aren't contacting the general's guards right now?"

"Are you afraid of another battle, Blaize?" Varian snipes from the other side of the room. "Don't want to get your blasters dirty?"

I shake my head. River and Varian have upped their snark toward Blaize ever since learning he's my mate too, but Blaize is taking it the way he takes everything, with a cool indifference that rivals even my stubbornness.

I kind of love that about him, just as much as I love River's endearing charm and Varian's monstrous attitude.

That hollow space inside me yawns awake—always at the most inopportune times—and I shift in my seat. I have three of the most amazing mates in the realms, but something is missing. I know what, but I don't dare even think it. It hurts too damn much.

"Battles I can handle," Blaize finally says. "It's the time wasted that bothers me. I don't like waiting and I don't like the opposing team having an upper hand on us."

"We don't know where these people stand," River says. "We can't condemn them as traitors before we've officially met their leader."

"You saw how the people were acting when we arrived," Varian chides him. "Skittish little things. You'd think we came with swords unsheathed and aimed at their throats."

"I agree," I say, and Varian smirks, nodding toward me. "With all of you," I clarify, and he cocks a brow at me. I blow out a breath, my head aching from all the thoughts, the strategies, the worry, the games. "They were acting skittish, but that could be because of the queen and her assassin's arrival. Plus, we know that the general already came through here—"

"And he left this city intact," Blaize interjects. "But not the neighboring one in the Slate Lands. The distress call that started us on this mission in the first place. Why leave this one untouched?"

My heart sinks and I nod. He's not wrong. The general laid waste to the neighboring villages in the Slate Lands, but the Onyx City is the most prestigious city the Isle has, save for my royal one. It's wealthy, chalked full of districts providing an array of supplies across the entire isle. It's one of the few cities that managed to rebuild itself into something new and unmatched after The Great War two centuries ago.

"The general likely left this one untouched because he wants their loyalty," I finally answer. "This city is a hub of wealth and provisions for the Shattered Isle. If his goal is to take my throne, it would be moronic of him to alienate his strongest ally."

"So you think the general bought them? Swayed them?" Blaize asks.

"I don't know," I say. "I agree with River that we need to give them a chance before we mark them as traitors to the crown."

A phantom weight settles around my brow. The crown I speak of is back at the palace, safe and protected for my return. I couldn't very well travel with it when trying to keep a low profile. And time is running out. If we intended to intercept the general and his guards as planned, then we need to move on by tomorrow, but I couldn't pass the Onyx City without uncovering where their loyalties lie.

Blaize's knee bounces where he sits next to me, his lips pursed. "I don't like it," he says. "To many what-ifs."

I smile softly at him, settling my hand over his leg. "Such is politics."

"I stopped playing into politics the moment I realized my previous king was sending me out to kill people who knew too much about his true self under the guise of them being enemies," Blaize says.

The bond between us chills inside me, as if his grief over his dark past crystalizes in a frost down our connection.

"Fucking stars," Varian says, stopping in the middle of his pacing.

River flashes Blaize a confused look as he presses off the wall, coming to sit in the chair opposite me and Blaize. "Is that what he made you do?" River asks, shock coloring his features. "That's why he cast you out?"

Blaize shrugs. "Once I refused to work for him anymore," he answers. "Talon and Tor thought I was spitting on the crown, betraying my kingdom. King Augustus couldn't kill me. He knew Steel would turn against him if he did, but the king did everything he could to ruin my standing in the All Plane." He shakes his head. "Steel was the only one who stood by my side."

"You never told him, did you?" River asks.

"The king threatened Steel's life if I ever told him the truth. I couldn't risk it, not before Steel and his brothers ascended the throne. And then after...after Augustus did what he did, I told him the truth. I knew Augustus was a piece of shit, but I never thought he'd turn on his sons the way he did. If I had been there..." His voice trails off, and River nods in agreement.

"We wish we all would've been there," he says. "He'd sent me and Storm so far across the realm there was no getting back in time. Where were you?"

"With Steel soaring off to the Shattered Isle, I had no reason to stay in the All Plane royal city until his return. I have a little secluded place on the far west of the All Plane. I go there to...process. I didn't know about Augustus's attack until I got back to prepare for Steel's return." He smacks his hands on his thighs before standing up, scanning the room. "So, that's why I don't play politics anymore, even with you, mate," he says, winking at me.

I swallow hard, my heart both full and breaking at the same time. Breaking for the past of my mate, breaking for the pain that has yet to heal for the All Plane or the Shattered Isle. Breaking for the unrest that has lived between our two Great Realms for centuries.

It's time for it to end.

Cari and me, we're that end. That change. Nothing is going to stop that, even traitorous cities or the general himself. I won't allow it.

"I always just thought you were a loose cannon," River admits, looking up at Blaize, who is now standing behind me, his restless energy hitting me in waves. "A rogue.

Someone who had a penchant for killing anyone who got in your way."

Blaize huffs a laugh. "Who is to say I'm not exactly what you think I am?"

I glance over my shoulder and up at Blaize, flashing him a chiding look. I know better. He may be deadly with an enormous amount of power rippling through his veins, but he's no random assassin who delights in innocent deaths.

"I'm sorry," River says. "For what I thought. I—"

"Don't," Blaize cuts him off. "We may be bound now through Gessi, but I don't need to get all emotional over it."

River smiles up at him, shrugging. "Just saying."

"Well, that was cute and soul-revealing," Varian says, crossing the room to join our little group. "But my senses are on edge. If the leader doesn't come in here in two minutes, I'm going to shift and—"

"I'm so sorry to keep you all waiting for so long," a voice cuts over Varian's as a striking male strides into the room.

He has rich black skin that is stretched over tons of muscle, evident under the long dark tunic with indigo details he wears over simple silver pants. His hair is midnight and inky, hanging in locks down to his shoulders, silver adornments on their ends. He flashes us a charming smile, but his golden eyes give away much more than the grin—there is a heap of knowledge and cunning beneath the elegant exterior, and quite a bit of power too from the way my own rises and wraps around me on instinct.

"Huxton Dale," I say, rising from my chair. My mates shift as I move, forming an intimidating unit behind me. "I've been wanting to meet you for quite some time," I say, reaching out my hand in a peaceful offering.

He slides his hand into mine, the calluses of a warrior scraping against my skin. He folds his other hand over the top of mine, dipping his forehead to our joined hands. "And I you, your majesty," he says, his voice warm and inviting. He releases me, nodding to each of my mates. "I truly am sorry for the delay. We weren't expecting your visit, and I was across the city, overseeing a new production of armor my engineers have been working on for over a year."

"Are you planning to launch an attack with this newly developed armor?" I ask, but I'm still smiling, still feeling him out.

He grins back at me, golden eyes darting between the three males behind me. "Can we sit?" he asks, motioning to the chairs surrounding and sleek table where I'd been seated moments before. "Please," he says after my mates have made no motion to move.

I nod, sliding into the chair first. River takes the seat on my right, Blaize on my left. Varian is content to stand behind me, outright glaring at Huxton as he claims the seat across the table from us.

"I want you to know," Huxton says, sliding his palm over the table. "Me and my people have always been loyal to the Shattered Isle rulers, even when we didn't always agree with their methods."

I tip my chin, silently indicating for him to continue.

"We're an ambitious people, I will admit that, but we have no motivations to rule anyone but ourselves," he continues. "We're peaceful, but formidable. We have the means for war, but don't seek it. As you can understand, I'm sure, your majesty, we do not want another Great War. We've worked too hard and too long to be a casualty in a political battle for power."

"There is no battle for power," I say. "I am the queen of the Shattered Isle and Cari is queen of the All Plane. Together, we're hoping to bring peace between the realms."

Huxton nods, smiling again. And I have to admit, it's breathtaking. Everything about the gorgeous male screams power and wisdom. "There is no questioning who the true ruler of the Shattered Isle is," he says. "Not for me or my people. We stand with you. We stand with Cari," he says, covering his broad chest with his hand. "I hope you believe me when I say that. Especially after what I'm about to tell you."

My stomach drops with those words, the hairs on my neck standing on end.

"The general and his guards passed through here," he says, eyes darting between me and my mates. "And as I'm sure you've noticed, he did not sack the city."

"We're aware," Blaize says from my side. I can feel the tension mounting between all three of my mates. Each bond is tightening, three chains rippling with adrenaline and alarm.

I breathe deeply, sending a calming breeze down each bond. I need my head clear before we jump to conclusions.

Huxton visibly swallows, leaning back in his chair. A shamed but solid sort of look fluttering over his features. "We, of course, told him our alliance was with him—"

Varian's shifted arm darts past my shoulder, stretching across the table and wrapping around Huxton's throat, lifting him from his chair.

"Varian!" I snap.

"You heard him, love," he argues, eyes on me.

Huxton's jaw flexes as he dangles above the chair before his arm darts to his side, returning with a gleaming dagger.

Blaize gets up so fast he knocks his chair over, him and River already leaping on the table in unison as they rush for Huxton.

"Stop!" I command, and everyone freezes. "Look," I say,

noting the sharp blade is only touching Varian's arm, not slicing through it.

Golden eyes find mine, silently imploring.

"Release him, Varian," I demand, and Varian instantly drops him, albeit a little angrily.

Huxton lands on his feet, using his free hand to rub at his neck as he catches his breath. He points the dagger at Varian, grinning as if he didn't nearly lose his head. "You've got a hell of a grip," he says. "And that power? Stars above, what a gift."

Varian cocks a brow at me, and Blaize and River climb off the table. We're all standing now, and my heart is racing, but I manage to keep my voice even.

"You had the advantage," I say. "Could've sliced Varian's arm right off—"

"It would've grown back," Varian says, and I silence him with a look.

"You didn't. Why?"

"Glad you noticed, your majesty," he says, righting his chair and dropping into it. All casual confidence that makes me wonder just how truly powerful this male is to not blink twice at my ruthless mate. "Like I was saying, the general gave me two options. Promise him my loyalty or he sacks my city. As I said before, I have no interest in watching my people bleed. Naturally, I told him I was on his side."

I reach out with my own power, testing his, sensing it. It's ancient, that's for sure, but it doesn't feel...dangerous. Not to me, anyway. It feels warm and inviting and truthful. My instincts settle into this sensation, but I keep my face even.

"But you claim to support my queen?" River says, skeptical. "How are we to know that you're not simply playing whichever side grants you the most peace?"

Huxton snaps his fingers, pointing at River. "I like this

one. He's clever. Suspicious, but clever." He sighs. "The Onyx City will always be loyal to the crown. The general doesn't have the crown and nor should he. If he ever attained it, that would be the first time the Onyx City would go into open war. King Jerrick had his faults, but he fooled most of us for decades with his proclamations of searching for peace between the realms. When he married Cari off to the All Plane princes, we thought his centuries-long quest had been fulfilled. We were wrong, but his treachery to the Isle brought about a hope we never knew we needed." Huxton looks to me. "*You.*"

"I may have lied to spare my city," he continues. "And I know how that sounds, how it looks. You have no reason to trust me, but I hope that you will. Just as I hope you'll put an end to the general's madness. He's killed hundreds in his rage. I would not add my people to the fire."

I nod, understanding washing through me. Too many cities and villages on my isle are being pressed against these impossible choices. Survival instincts are hard to ignore, and if bending the knee spares a blade to the neck, what option would I choose?

"You love your people," I say, and Huxton nods.

"They've been mine for a long time," he says. "I would sooner sever my own head than watch them fall prey to the general and his soldiers."

I glance at River, then Varian. They're skeptical still, but I can see the softening in their gazes. They're leaning toward the side of believing him, but after everything we've been through, it's difficult to give him our full faith. Still, there is something about him I find trustworthy. He could've lied. Could've kept the information from us about his actions when the general was here, but he didn't. That has to count for something.

Blaize shifts to stand before me, pinning me with just a look as he nods almost imperceptibly. Relief trickles into my veins like tendrils of warmth. My mate has a knack for sniffing out when someone is untrustworthy, but only if he hears the lie aloud. Had Blaize been in the meeting with me and Trince, we likely could've avoided the betrayal. I won't make that mistake again.

"I'm choosing to believe you," I say when Blaize has moved to face Huxton again.

Huxton releases a breath.

"Thank you, your majesty. I know that isn't easy."

"Nothing about being queen is easy," I say, my heart still heavy from everything that has happened in the last few days.

"Maybe I can return this trust," he says, and I raise my brows at him. He leans over the table, eyes darting between each of us. "You trust my words and I'll trust you to take the right action with them."

"I'm listening," I say.

"I know where the general is," he says. "And it's not where you think."

16

GESSI

"How do you know?" Varian asks as we all lean over the table, eyes on the map Huxton has spread out over it.

Huxton taps his temple. "It's a gift," he says. "Hard to explain."

Blaize cuts an icy glare at him at the same time Varian huffs, "Not a good enough explanation."

Huxton turns those golden eyes on me. "Are they this skeptical of everyone?"

I can't help but laugh. "Yes," I say, motioning toward the map. "We were going to intercept him here," I say, pointing to Sand's Swallow.

Huxton nods. "I see how you would think that's his next location," he says. "Especially after traveling through the Slate Lands." He drags his finger over a city closer to his— Jasmine Falls—and taps it. "But this is where he'll be the night after next."

"Again," Varian growls. "How do you know that?"

Huxton sighs, pushing off the table, pressing his palms together like he's searching for patience. For the first time since he's entered the room, I can see another side of him, a dangerous, powerful side. A direct opposition to his calm, charming demeanor, but it doesn't unnerve me in the way Trince's behavior did. This seems more of a logical reaction to Varian's constant probing, and I have to wonder just how much more there is to the Onyx City ruler that rumbles beneath the surface.

"How can you shift into...whatever it is that you are?"

Varian parts his lips, then closes them.

"Exactly," Huxton says. "One of my many gifts is seeing across far distances, not with my eyes but with my mind. If I focus hard enough, I can even pinpoint our dear Cari."

"Really?" I ask. "Then what is she doing right this second?"

Huxton straightens, his churning gilded eyes going distant despite looking directly at me. A few moments of silence pass before a grin shapes his lips, and he blinks quickly. "She's doing something I most certainly shouldn't be spying on," he says, and I laugh, knowing he's likely right.

I mean, it's what *I'd* be doing if I didn't have the weight of an impending war sitting on my shoulders. If I had time and space to explore my mates, get to know them on the deepest of levels, that's exactly what I'd be doing.

If.

But I don't live in that world right now, and if Cari knew what I'm going through? She'd be here faster than I could tell her not to come. And I will not rob her of that peace she's earned. I will not make her regret her decision, make her abandon her new throne to come help me protect mine.

"Fine," Varian grumbles. "If you can do this, then why didn't you seal the city before the general arrived?"

"I'm not psychic," Huxton argues. "You think I have time to keep tabs on everyone across the realms?" He shakes his head. "I didn't know he was coming," he continues. "And even now, he's hard to pinpoint."

River raises his hands, clearly at the end of his rope. "But you just said—"

"I know what I said," Huxton cuts him off. "The general's power, his ability to be invisible, to move things with his mind, it's making his signature hard to pinpoint. I catch glimpses, but sometimes he's too far away, even when he's not."

"So we may go here in two days," Blaize says, pointing to Jasmine Falls on the map. "And he may not be there?"

"Yes," Huxton admits. "But, for now, that's what his plan is. I sought him earlier, and that's where he was ordering his guards." He glances between my mates, incredulous. "It's better than you lot marching to Sand's Swallow in the completely wrong direction!"

"He has a point," I say, and all eyes turn to me. "I'd rather risk missing him at a spot he's more likely to be, than waste nights going where he won't."

Blaize touches my elbow, drawing me away from the table. River and Varian follow. "That's if you trust him," Blaize whispers.

"I can hear you," Huxton says, folding his arms behind his back. "But, carry on."

A muscle in Blaize's jaw flexes.

"We're with you," River says. "Whatever you decide."

Varian gives a curt nod, one that Blaize mimics.

And somehow, that support has me filling with warmth and love and gratitude and at the same time...*uncertainty*.

Because Crane...he'd likely be telling me to be more cautious, strategize better. He'd tell me to trust my instincts, but sharpen my mind. He'd...

He isn't here. And that hollow space in my heart gets a

little larger each day that I don't see him. Despite everything between us, I *know* what that means.

I can't bear to know what that means.

I wonder if he's made it back to the palace yet, if he's bothered to check in with Lance at all while he's there.

"What's it going to be, love?" Varian asks, shaking me to the present.

"In two nights' time, we'll take out the general and his guards at Jasmine Falls."

"Marvelous," Huxton says, clapping his hands together. "We should celebrate, yes?"

"I don't think that's necessary," I say, waving him off as he rounds the table toward us. "We'll need to prepare and rest for the upcoming battle."

"Of course," Huxton says. "But part of that preparation is a stiff drink and a good meal, wouldn't you agree?" he asks, clapping Varian on the back so hard the evidence of his shift ripples across his face. Huxton roars with laughter, a deep belly laugh that is contagious.

"A meal doesn't sound too bad," I admit.

"Excellent," Huxton says, extending his hand toward me. "If you three don't mind, I'm going to steal your mate for the first portion of the evening. Give her a proper tour of my estate."

Blaize shifts toward me, Varian and River following.

"It's fine," I say, nearly blushing at the possessive looks on each of their faces. "How could you tell?" I ask, turning back to Huxton as he leads me out of the room.

"You can practically smell the mating bonds between the three of you," he says, and I laugh.

"Do you have one of your own?" I ask.

"No," he says quickly. "For several reasons, but not for lack of those trying." He sighs. "Being the leader of the

second largest city on the Isle is a draw for some only inter-
ested in the position and the rest are too afraid to get near
me because of my power." A half-grin shapes his lips as he
looks down at me. "Who would want a mate who can spy on
them no matter how far they run?"

My heart dips at the notion and I'm tempted to spare a
glance over my shoulder at my mates. They've never feared
my power and never coveted my crown, but I can see where
Huxton would have issue with uncovering whose intentions
would be real with him and whose wouldn't.

"You never know," I say, genuinely wanting to give him
hope. I never thought what happened to me was possible,
never knew this kind of happiness and love was possible
before my assassins found me. "It would be worth the risk to
me," I continue. "Sifting through the bad and the good until
you find the *true*. I wouldn't lose hope."

Huxton turns down a long hallway decorated with
artwork depicting the Isle's villages and cities, all framed in
gold. "Hope is an easy thing to lose," he says. "Especially
when time has proven over and over again to be
unyielding."

I tilt my head from side to side, unable to argue with
him, but still hopeful for him all the same. Even now, as he
leads me through his massive estate, pointing out artwork or
historical artifacts, educating me on the rich history of the
Onyx City, I can *feel* all three of my mates trailing not far
behind.

And that kind of support and love and dedication is
something I feel everyone deserves.

"What do you think of my city, your majesty?" Huxton asks me, hours later, as we sit in a room filled with his people, eating, drinking, dancing. Many of them have already stopped by my table to say their thanks and their hopes for my reign.

"It's truly beautiful," I say, clinking my goblet against his. The sparkling wine has done wonders to soothe my frayed nerves, not to mention the feast Huxton had provided for us.

"I'm quite proud of it," he says, glancing around at his people who are filling his banquet hall in his estate. There is such love in his eyes, such a sense of pride, but beyond that I can see something more...something...sad, maybe, but I can't quite put my finger on it.

Again, I don't fear it. Not like I had with Trince and the way he behaved. After spending the evening with Huxton, I feel I've gained an irreplaceable ally—but, as I've already learned the hard way, I know only time will tell.

After another hour of talking and dancing and eating, I'm more than ready to retire for the evening. "I have to thank you again," I say, rising from the table and leaning over to grip Huxton's hand. "I'm grateful for your hospitality." And the information, I add silently. I know he can't read my mind, but I hope he can at least read my eyes.

"Forever and always, my queen," he says, sweeping his goblet to indicate the room. "My city is yours whenever you have need of it."

"I will take you up on that sometime."

He grins up at me. "I'll show you even more tomorrow evening," he says. "We've only scratched the surface."

I smile at him, nodding before I head out of the room, my mates on my heels. After shutting the door to the generous room Huxton offered us for the next two evenings, I blow out a breath.

"Too much socializing, love?" Varian asks, the first one to stand before me. He knows me to my core, knows how being around a crowd too long can just zap my energy levels.

"Maybe," I say. I *am* tired and with dawn approaching, I know we need to rest for what little time we can. I smooth my hand over Varian's cheek before glancing behind him at Blaize and River. "We only have a few hours," I say, and identical confused looks cross their faces. "We're leaving today."

"What?" River asks.

"In the daylight?" Varian groans.

Blaize merely smirks, a flicker of pride rippling down our bond. "Clever queen."

Warmth spreads over my skin at his praise. "Yes, in the daylight," I answer Varian first.

"But you told Huxton we wouldn't be leaving until the night after tomorrow," River says, then realization washes over his features.

"You're testing him," Varian says, nodding.

"I trust him," I clarify. "But he's so close with his people, even the staff here know of our plans. If someone leaks the information, I want to maintain the upper hand. We leave in a few hours and get to Jasmine Falls before the general and his guards arrive. If they storm in prepared for an ambush, we know someone betrayed us. And if not..."

"Then we'll have maintained the upper hand by having the best vantage point," Blaize finishes for me.

"Exactly." I look at him and then River. "Plus, you two could use some time in the sun, right?"

"It would help," River says. "I haven't spent as much time in it as I should."

"Neither have I," Blaize says. "Not since..."

"Since you accepted the bond," I say, smiling at him. "New rule," I say, and he cocks a brow at me. "You two dedicate real time to refilling your energy stores in the sun, just as Varian and I will in the stars. I can't have either of you weakened simply because you don't want to leave my side."

Blaize crosses his arms over his chest. "Since when do you give me orders?"

I bite my bottom lip. "Just this once," I say, and he smirks at me.

"Fine," he agrees.

"Of course, my queen," River says, and flames lick my skin at the way all of them are looking at me.

Each one has a different way of making me feel wanted and loved and *stars* it's consuming sometimes. The bonds between each of us pulses with heat and need. River tugs me into his arms, sliding his mouth over mine in a tender, loving kiss that makes me sigh in contentment.

Then Varian is at my back, kissing down my neck, and Blaize? *Stars*, Blaize is there too, that silver arm wrapping around my waist, his hand exploring lower, until we're nothing but a beautiful tangle of tongues and teeth and hands and bodies.

17

GESSI

Blaize's fingers are powerful as he slides them between my heat, and I rock against them, tingles rushing over my body from how strong they are, almost like warm, smooth steel is teasing me.

River's kiss turns carnal, a claiming of my mouth that steals my breath.

And Varian? Stars, he's partially shifted, sliding that long, slightly rough tongue down my back as he helps me out of my gown. Helps everyone out of their clothes without interrupting our connection for long.

I know we should be sleeping, should be resting in preparation for the journey to come. Moving under daylight will cover us, but it will exhaust Varian and I. And if someone here betrays us? The general will have the upper hand, and I of all creatures know what he does when he gains the upper hand.

Torture and death.

The mere *idea* of my mates being harmed is enough to make my stomach sour, but if the general gets his hands on them?

A shudder runs the length of my body, spurring me to kiss River harder, rock against Blaize greedily, and reach back to grip Varian's hair with a stinging hold.

I can't lose them. My soul and theirs are braided in a way that losing one would be like losing a piece of myself.

But I know the odds we're walking into.

Maybe that's why I'm not ordering us all to sleep.

Maybe that's why I'm clinging to them with greedy touches, claiming kisses, and desperate need.

I will give and take and take and give every last drop of love and passion between us until they know and feel how important they are to me.

Heat pools low in my core as Blaize ups his pace, accelerating his fingers so fast they're almost vibrating against my flesh. My body tightens, my orgasm building—

Blaize withdraws his fingers so fast my head spins, and seconds later I'm being hauled away from River's mouth, my face turned an inch away from Blaize's.

"Not yet," he says, and I whimper before he crushes his lips against mine.

"Greedy mate," Varian growls, but there is humor even in his partially shifted voice. "Aww, you look lonely, pretty boy," he continues, and I can't help but peek at them.

"What are you going to do about it?" River asks, motioning his head in challenge to Varian.

I sigh into Blaize's mouth, my heart racing from his kiss. Stars, he's like a shot of pure adrenaline and danger. His tongue slides into my mouth with a primal need that has my toes curling against the floor. My entire being is sparking, crackling with tension, hanging on the edge right where Blaize wants me.

"Fuck," Varian growls, and I spare another look while digging my fingers into the muscles of Blaize's arms.

And my body twists and coils at the sight, all delicious warm tendrils as I watch Varian and River crash together, their muscled bodies pressed against each other as they kiss. I break our kiss long enough to turn Blaize's head, dropping slowly to my knees before him. Wrapping my lips around his hard cock, sucking him into my mouth while he watches Varian and River.

Those winter eyes are searing with interest and desire too as he grips my hair and thrusts into my mouth. He's all heat and strength as I bob up and down on him, my eyes flickering from him to Varian and River and back. My body a string of need as I devour him, savor him—

Blaize gently tugs my hair, pulling out of my mouth with a devious smile that has my lips parting as he hauls me to my feet, effortlessly sliding that silver arm beneath my ass and hefting me to his eye level.

Stars, how is he so strong? How are each of them? How did I get this lucky?

A sliver of dread sluices through my veins at the idea of losing this newfound bliss—at the thought of what I *know* is missing. My heart is fuller than it's ever been, my soul on the cusp of completion in a way I never imagined, and it only increases the fear of losing that fullness ten times more.

"Stay with me," Blaize demands, his dominant tone ripping me out of the spiral. I lock eyes with him, wrapping my arms around his neck as I study the flecks of white in his wintry blue eyes. "Stay with us," he continues, that authoritative tone reaching across the room.

"I'm here," I promise him, willing my mind to stay in the present, to not wander one second beyond the next.

"Good," Blaize says, nipping at my bottom lip. "Lock your ankles."

I do as I'm told, and Blaize shifts, sliding his cock through my heat. I tremble at the sensation, my flesh so sensitive from the edge he left me on moments ago. "Blaize," I sigh, my thighs clenching around his hips as he holds me to him.

His eyes hold mine for a second before he looks behind me and nods almost imperceptibly, as if someone asked him for permission to do something. And then River is there, at my back, kissing my neck and sliding his hands down my back, over where Blaize holds me.

And Varian, *stars,* Varian drops to his knees beside us, sliding that shifted tongue of his over River's cock, making it slick. Varian's hands are on my thighs while Blaize still teases me, and it's a whirl of sensation that sweeps me into an orbit I never want to end.

"Fuck, River," Varian growls. "You even taste like the sun," he says, swirling that tongue all around his cock, up and down his shaft, until River's fingers are gripping my hips tight. Varian smirks up at all three of us, rising from his kneeled position as he nods to River. "Slide it in her ass," he says to River. "You won't believe how good her ass is at taking a cock."

The words are filthy, but they don't make me feel dirty. Not here, in Blaize's arms, River at my back, Varian watching with a predator's gaze, as if he's searching for the next place to strike any one of us.

River steps even closer, until his chest presses against my back, my chest against Blaize's, and he rubs the head of his cock over that tight, sensitive spot. He's slick from Varian, all warm and sweet as he teases me.

Warm tendrils quiver in my blood as Blaize teases me from the front and River from behind. I'm suspended between the two, held effortlessly as they both take my weight.

"You like that, my queen?" River whispers in my ear, slipping his cock in an inch before pulling it out.

"Yes," I groan as Blaize does the same thing from the front.

"She wants you to fuck her," Blaize says. "Don't you, mate?"

I nod, biting on my bottom lip to keep from moaning again. The two of them, *stars* I can barely breathe—

Blaize thrusts inside my heat in one smooth motion, filling me, sending jolts of electricity crackling across my skin. He shudders as he holds me there, feeling my heat adjust around his size. "She's so fucking warm," Blaize says, to River or to Varian, I'm not sure.

"Let's see," River says, and slides home, the ease made smoother because of Varian's mouth.

I gasp at the sensation, sandwiched between the two as they take their time sliding in and out until they find a rhythm that has them moving in sync.

I can't do anything but hold on, my thighs tight around Blaize's hips, my head leaned back against River's broad shoulder as I watch them have their way with me. My body is clenching around them both, all warm shivers and breathy moans and then Varian is there, on the other side of us, slanting his mouth over mine—no shift, just him.

Varian's kiss is searing while Blaize's thrusts are unrelenting and River's are smooth and steady. The contrast whirls and twists and twines inside my body, awakening needs and desires in me that were only ever going to be fulfilled by them.

Each of them.

They were made for me and me for them.

I reach up with one hand, still clinging to Blaize with the other, and tangle my fingers in Varian's hair.

"I want to taste your mouth when you come, love," he whispers against my lips, smirking as his eyes move to Blaize and River and back again. Watching them fuck me. Watching them work my body up and up until I feel I might combust from the consuming heat of it all.

They're keeping me on the cusp on purpose, the bastards. In true assassin form, they're content to draw out the torture until I'm sure Varian can taste it on my tongue, the desperation to be shoved over that edge and fly.

River uses his free hand to grip Varian's cock, making him growl against my mouth as he thrusts into River's hand.

"Stars," I gasp against Varian's mouth, trembling as Blaize and River up their pace. "Mates," I groan, unable to form more words beyond that. "*Mates.*" The word is both a plea and a promise as I send every sensation, every emotion down our bonds.

They groan in response, each different and distinct, their sounds like a signature I could understand even from miles away.

Mine.

They're mine.

"I..." I gasp, my thighs trembling as Blaize pounds into me, pushing me right up to the knife's-edge of my orgasm. "I..."

River matches Blaize's pace, stealing my thoughts, my breath, but I cling to what I need to say by some shred of a miracle.

"I love you," I say, breathless. I want them to know, *need* them to know.

"Fucking love you," Varian growls into my mouth, then demands, "*harder*," to River.

"Love my queen," River says, his chest flexing against my back.

Blaize meets my eyes, slowing his thrusts so much I whimper as he drags out the precursor, squeezing every last drop of desperation out of me until I feel like I'm floating in a sea of need. A sea *he* controls.

He doesn't have to say anything, doesn't have to part his lips. His eyes tell me everything, that silvery bond between us glowing and pulsing with the love he doesn't give word to. I gasp from the intensity in that sensation, in what he pours down the bond while he unleashes himself on me. Pumping and pounding into me so fast that River has to hang on to me with one hand so I stay connected to him.

Again and again, Blaize takes my body, devours it whole as River adjusts behind me, Varian stealing every last breath as they all work me into a frenzy—

"Stars!" I cry out as my body explodes into a thousand pieces of glittering starlight. Searing heat cascades down my spine, making my entire body quake as I come. I clench around Blaize and River so tightly as the shocks keep coming in waves, my eyes rolling back in my head as Varian groans against my mouth, his tongue sliding over mine as I shiver with delight.

Blaize growls, hardening another degree as he spills inside me, River not a second behind him. Varian tenses against my mouth, his own orgasm warm against my thigh where River holds him.

We stand there, an unbreakable unit of love and passion, catching our breath for a few heartbeats before my mates set to work. Gently shifting out of me, one gathering what we need to clean up, the other carrying me to the bed, and the last getting all of us water. It's effortless and beautiful, to the point I feel like my heart is overflowing, like it's too big to fit inside my chest.

And when we all settle into bed, I can't tell where one begins and the other ends, and I am fine with that for the rest of forever.

18

GESSI

Brushstrokes of orange and pink and lavender smear across the sky by the time we make it to Jasmine Falls. The smell of night-blooming flowers hangs in the air, the sound of the crashing natural falls is loud even from a few miles away.

I'm exhausted from walking beneath the sun all day and from the lack of sleep we had prior to leaving the Onyx City. We left Varian's sky-ship docked in the city, not wanting to give anyone the chance to know we're coming.

Blaize and River look ready for battle, their eyes sharp and bodies upright, where Varian and I definitely have seen better nights.

"Is this how you two feel all the time?" I ask Blaize and River once we've reached the outskirts of the village, pausing to catch our breath on a bank of flat stones that litter the pathway toward the main roads. "Living under the stars with me?" I take the water River offers, gulping it down before handing it to Varian.

The notion hurts my heart, wondering why the fates

would pair us as mates if we're weakened under each other's preferred sky.

"No, my queen," River says, kneeling to be at my eye level. He smooths his hand over my cheek. "It's easy to replenish my energy and power once a week under the sun. You are wiped out because of lack of sleep and exerting your powers at every turn. These aren't normal circumstances. You know that. Even Cari adjusted to living under the sun."

I nod, the tension in my chest easing with his words.

"He's right," Blaize backs him up. "The sun is not to blame for zapping you," he continues. "This journey is."

"But it's worth it," I say, the water doing wonders for my muscles. Blaize and River are right—I've been pushing myself harder and harder each day. Pulling on my reserves of power sometimes just to stay upright. The constant worrying and strategizing and battles have taken their toll on my body, making me restless—a feeling of dread swirling in my stomach I just can't shake. With each step we get closer, the more terror awakens inside me. I try to shove it down, try to surmise it to worrying over my mates, but it's hard to ignore.

"When this is over," I say, rising from where I'd been sitting. "I would like to sleep for a week." I glance at each of them. "Can I do that?" I ask sheepishly.

"You are queen," River says. "You can do whatever you want."

"Stars no, you can't," Varian says. "I've got lost time to make up for." He winks at me, and I laugh, the sensation chasing away my incessant fear.

"We'll allow you to rest," Blaize says. "When we're done with you."

My smile deepens, my energy invigorated by their teasing, their primal need for me and me for them.

"When we get home," Varian says, stalking toward me like the apex predator he is. "I'm going to—"

The roar of a sky-ship cuts him off and he whirls around, shifting partially as we all look to the skies.

"Huxton sold us out," Blaize growls.

I reach for his silver arm, gently gripping it. "No," I say, watching the direction of the sky-ship. "Look. It's not coming for us. It doesn't know we're here."

"Shit," Blaize spits once he realizes I'm right. "They're early."

I nod. "And they're going for the village."

BLAIZE and I are breathless by the time we reach the entrance to the village. My side aches from running so hard and fast, but Varian in his shifted form and River in his shrunken size have already beaten us.

Screams ring out like warning bells, the general's favorite anthem. The sky-ship has landed, dominating the Jasmine Falls docking zone, and over twenty guards spill from the ship's belly.

Guards wearing the previous Shattered Isle uniform, with one distinct change—instead of the moon and stars being the emblem across the chest, it's a perfect rendering of the general's sunken-in face, his razor-sharp teeth on display, all in tones of silver and blood-red.

My blood runs cold as the last three remaining on the ship debark.

Erix and a guard I don't recognize.

And the general himself.

Blaize notes the panic rippling down our bond, likely flashing in my eyes as I watch the two scan the area. He reaches over, gently gripping my arm, spinning me to look him in the eye.

"The one with him," Blaize says, jerking his head across the way to where Erix and the general are barking orders at the guards.

The residents of Jasmine Falls look as if they were preparing for a market evening before the sky-ship arrived. Fruits and vegetables and bundled herbs have been left forgotten in their wooden crates, some overturned as the people flee from the guard's swords.

"Is he the one?" Blaize asks.

The breath in my lungs is too tight.

I can't get enough air in.

Memories flash like sparks from a blaster behind my eyes—Erix's claws slicing into me, nearly killing me. The general's blades sinking into me enough to hurt and to bleed, but not merciful enough for death.

"Gessi," he demands, and a jolt of icy strength soars down our bond.

"Yes," I say. "Erix. It's Erix."

Blaize's entire face shifts—not like Varian's star's-given power, but in a brutally beautiful way. A horrifying way. He's death incarnate as he turns away from me, his icy eyes set on Erix across the village.

"He's mine," he growls, sparing a glance over his shoulder. "Come claim what's yours," he orders, nodding toward the general.

The panic crackling in my veins melts with the searing strength he sends down our bond. I'm no longer chained to the walls of the palace dungeon. No longer bound by the damn stone that drained my powers and made me helpless against their torture.

I am queen of the Shattered Isle, and General Payne will

spill blood on my soil no more.

I draw on my power as I take the first step, that decisive move opening up my lungs and flooding me with much-needed air. Varian and River fight four of the general's guards each to my left and right, taking blows meant for innocent lives.

Fighting for people they've never met.

Fighting for my queendom.

They're relentless as I up my pace, now running toward the object of all my nightmares. The reason for the panic that has hindered me these last months. The terror that has gripped my soul for far too long. If my mates can fight without hesitance, without fear, then so can I.

I hurry along a cobblestoned path, my eyes set on the general, who is standing at the base of the ship, smirking at the battle raging before him.

Not even a battle, a *massacre*.

That's what this is, what this very well would be if we hadn't left the Onyx City early. If we hadn't been here.

A guard slams into my path, knocking me back a few inches. I draw on my power, gathering the dirt beneath the stones at my feet, and send it soaring down his throat before he can even raise his sword. He claws at his neck, trying to rid himself of the suffocating earth before he falls to the ground.

Cries for help sing out to my right—a female is standing before three younglings, her body the only thing standing between the guard stalking toward them and her children. She's fearless as she stares him down, even as he swipes his sword at her. Teasing her, playing with his would-be kill.

I dig my feet into the ground, racing that direction, vines snapping and twisting at my side as I curl my fingers. I leash one thick, prickly vine around the guard's ankle and yank.

His gut slams into the stones before the female, and I drag him away from them.

"Run!" I say, breathless, as I continue to haul the monster toward me with my vines.

The female's eyes fill with gratitude before she wrangles her crying younglings and hurries them down the street where the fighting is minimal before ducking into a building.

"Bitch usurper," the guard spits as he flails, flipping over to his back. He slices through the vine at his ankle, leaping to his feet in a heartbeat.

He's twice my size, thicker in the middle, and has spit rolling down his cheek. I have to crane my neck to look up at him.

"The general is going to tear you apart when I bring you to him," he says, backhanding me with the hilt of his sword so fast I don't have time to dodge.

I sputter as the wind is knocked from me and I nearly losing my footing before I regain my balance. My cheek is on fire from the hit, but I straighten, curling my fingers.

"One hit," he says. "That's for me. But you try anything again and I'll kill you instead of handing you over to the general."

I smirk at him, working my vines behind him, growing and stretching them while he runs his mouth. "I'll see myself to him, but thanks," I say, and draw my hands together in front of my chest.

Instantly, vines leash his wrists and ankles, tight enough to crush bone.

"No!" he screams as my vines slowly, agonizingly stretch his limbs in opposite directions. "No! Please! No!"

I step up to him, tilting my head. "Have you *ever* listened to those pleas of mercy?" I ask, voice cold as ice.

His eyes widen.

"Me either." I rip my hands away from each other, the motion directing my vines to soar...and his limbs snap off his body along with them.

I spare no thought to the brutal scene as I spin on my heels. Varian and River and Blaize are fighting their way through the guards, dropping them one by one like the elite assassins they are, but even I can see the exhaustion in their bodies.

Blaize is like a deadly machine as he finishes one guard, then another, barely even looking at them as he cracks their necks with that silver arm of his. His eyes are only on Erix, and mine are on the male next to him. The one watching as his guards bleed to death with nothing but amusement on his face.

It sends icy terror through me, but I push myself harder, faster, until I skid to a stop not five feet from him, power crackling between my palms.

"General Payne," I say in a deathly cold voice.

His eyes slice to mine and the amusement deepens on his face. "Little flower," he says, and I cringe at the nickname. "You've turned my favorite pet into nothing more than a whipped dog." He nods behind me, where Varian is finishing the last of the guards, his massive obsidian form dominating the space.

"He's always been mine," I spit back. Adrenaline surges in my veins as I study the general, looking for the best place to attack. He's not like the guards, he won't go down easy. And with his power? He can blink out of sight at any second or send a dagger straight to my heart with half a thought.

Smart.

I have to be smart.

Blaize skids to a halt on my left, looking to me for the

plan. I motion for him to hold, almost imperceptible to anyone else.

"What do you gain from this, General?" I ask, hoping to get him talking. He loves to talk. I learned that in my cell while he tortured me. "Killing these defenseless people? Attacking these peaceful villages across the Isle?"

Payne folds his hands behind his back, considering. The blades on his belt glimmer under the last rays of the setting sun, and the scars beneath my fighting leathers prickle with the memory of their sting.

"That's the question, isn't it, Little Flower?" He curls his lips at me. "King Jerrick would've known immediately what I was doing."

Dread fills my stomach, weighing my powers down for a heartbeat.

"That's one reason, and there are many, why you shouldn't be queen," he continues. "You have no vision. No mind for strategy. A female never does."

Erix laughs at his side as the other guard comes to stand on the opposite side of the general, forming a protective unit around him.

But it's just them now.

Just Erix and the general and one guard.

We can finish this.

Hope blooms in my chest, a rush of power sliding over me as I draw upon as much of it as I possess.

"You're outnumbered," I say, feeling River shifting to normal size at my back, and Varian, in his beautiful, monstrous form. And in that moment, when I feel their support, I wish Crane was here. Despite all the hate, all the pain, I wish he was here to see this. To be part of us finishing it. "And you're done playing whatever sick game it is you're trying to play."

Payne laughs this time. "Little Flower, you have no idea who you're playing with."

"Don't I?" I say, directing my power to the stones beneath his boots. I have to be quick. I have to ensure I'm controlling every ounce of rock and dirt beneath him, and bury him twice as fast. "You're the one who delights in torturing, but only when it's in your favor. Only when you have powers leashed by those disgusting chains you concocted—"

"Ah," he cuts me off. "Interesting you should mention that." He turns to Erix and with one look, Erix raises a blaster and fires directly at Blaize.

I'm too slow.

Blaize is too slow.

And it hits him—

"Blaize!" I scream, everything narrowing as he drops to his knees. He palms his chest, but he's not bleeding. It's a needle...a needle in his chest...

His eyes go wide. "My...power..."

Two more blasts fly past my face so fast I feel the wind on my face.

Varian and River go down.

Varian immediately shifts to his normal form. River is splayed out on his back, unconscious.

"Fuck," Varian hisses, ripping the needle out of his chest. "You right bastard!" he growls.

I flick my fingers, the ground trembling at the general's feet. He sinks an inch before Erix shoots me, the needle piercing the skin at the base of my throat.

I wobble on my feet, the world spinning for half a second as my vision goes blurry. Everything inside me shuts down, those pathways to my power feel like they're being slammed behind steel doors and sealed with locks.

Just like the fucking chains he used to keep me in.

"*This*?" I spit, my vision clearing. "This is what you've been doing? Testing a new concoction?"

"Among other things, Little Flower," he says as Erix helps him out of the sunken earth. He shakes the dirt off his boots, eying me. "That wasn't very nice."

I bare my teeth at him, feeling like my muscles are made of rubber. I hunch over a bit, the bonds between me and my mates flickering and gasping for breath from the poison in our veins.

Stars, don't let this be permanent. Please wear off. Wear off!

Payne saunters past me, spitting on the ground before Varian. "Waste of space," he says through his teeth before walking back to me. "You were my favorite," he says, still looking at Varian. He glances around, eyes scanning the rooftops of the surrounding buildings. "Where is Crane? Has he had the decency enough to leave you in the dust?" he considers, sliding his tongue along those spindly teeth. "I always liked him. Well, except for his slight lapse in judgment when you were in the cells."

I tilt my head, and he shakes his head. "You really don't know anything do you, Little Flower?" His chest expands with a prideful breath. "Crane didn't like me and Erix playing with you. It didn't sit right with him, the things we were doing. He went to your cell, prepared to free you. Help you escape. We caught him before he was successful." A malicious grin stretches his face, and Erix grunts approval from behind him. Payne crouches down to catch my eyes. "We didn't hurt him, you know," he says. "Not physically. We simply...*used* his sentiment against him. His affections for you were pathetic. He needed to learn his lesson. I ordered him to stand guard every night, to watch what Erix so adoringly did to you, and if Crane stepped a toe out of line? Well, then I would've had to *unleash* Erix on you."

Tears well behind my eyes at his words, angry and hurt and lost.

Payne laughs again. "You didn't really think what Erix was doing to you was the *worst* he could've done, do you?"

Icy dread slides over me as I glance to Erix. There is nothing in his eyes, nothing but malicious, disgusting evil.

"Honestly, I practically dared him to defy me. Poor Erix was counting on it," Payne continues. "Crane deserved the punishment. Fitting for his crimes. The mental torture was delicious. You could almost see the sanity chip away in his eyes every single night." He shrugs. "Oh well, Erix will have plenty of time to fulfil *those* needs when you come with us."

"I'm not going anywhere with you," I spit, forcing myself to straighten.

"Touch her and die," Blaize says, struggling to stand from the poison. He manages to raise his silver arm, pointing at Erix.

Erix smirks. "I'm going to do more than touch her," he says. "I'm going to *ruin* her in every way imaginable until there is nothing but a shell left for you to fuck."

"Your head," Varian growls. "I'm going to tear it from your shoulders."

"Corner," Payne calls, completely unphased by the threats. The second guard hurries to his side. "Contain the little flower, would you?"

The guard snatches me up, holding me with one arm wrapped around my chest as I struggle against him. "Keep doing that," he says at my ear. "I like it."

I go wholly still and he moves his bulging arm to my throat, putting just enough pressure there to keep me in place. I reach for my powers once again, but only hit those horrific steel doors. He drags me back to the base of the ship, forcing me to look at the sight of my mates on their knees.

Payne stalks before my mates, pointing at each as he goes. "Who should be the first to die?"

I gasp, struggling again. Doing my best to break free.

This isn't happening.

This *can't* be happening.

Payne turns to me, his clawed finger still trailing over each of my mates as he walks back and forth. "Who is your favorite?" he asks, and I glare at him, tears spilling over my lashes. "Perhaps I'll let that one live, if you agree to cooperate."

"Just take me," I beg. "Kill me. Let them go. *Please.*" I'm begging now.

I'm begging the male who tortured me and my queendom for months and I don't care. I'll do anything for my mates. Anything to save them.

"Kill you?" Payne tsks me. "Little Flower, I have no interest in killing you. You're too valuable an asset. Just think how the traitorous whore of an All Plane queen will bend to me, knowing that your life hangs in the balance? *Again.*"

I close my eyes, tears rolling down my cheeks.

Cari.

I've failed not only my mates, but Cari too.

How the hell did I get here? How did I let this horrible monster outsmart me?

"No favorite?" he asks again, walking the line, pointing at each. "Very well, then." He shrugs, heading back toward me. "Erix, do the beast first. He's wounded me the most with his treachery."

Erix clambers over to Varian, who tries to fight him, but is too weakened by the poison. Erix grips Varian's hair in one hand and presses a dagger to his throat with the other.

My heart is breaking.

Cracking.

Fracturing into a thousand pieces.

And I'm screaming, thrashing against the guard holding me, all while the general *laughs*.

"Take your time with them, Erix," he says, heading into the sky-ship. "Bring her to me when you're done. Alive," he commands. "I'll send your friends to pick you up when you're done playing. You've earned it. I have a throne to take." He disappears into the ship, the loading dock closing after him. Minutes later, the thing catapults into the sky, soaring in the direction of my palace.

"Varian," I cry, clawing at the guard's arm.

"Do that again and I'll cut his eyes out first," Erix snaps.

I go still.

Corner squeezes me tighter, pressing his cheek to mine. "Watch," he says. "Erix's an artist when it comes to this. But you know that better than me, don't you?"

I cringe against his hold, silently begging the stars, the sun, whatever higher powers exist to spare my mates. Take my life, subject me to whatever tortures lay ahead, but *spare* them.

"It's all right, love," Varian whispers, his words reaching me across the distance. "It'll be all right."

I shake my head, my soul splintering as Erix smirks at me, toying with me as he holds that dagger to Varian's throat.

River is laid out next to Varian, barely able to raise his head from the poison, and Blaize, on his knees, still attempting to rise over and over again but failing every time.

Even in the face of death, they're still trying to comfort me, to get to me, to protect me, and they can't...

This...this can't be how we end.

The general can't win.

He can't.

I gather all my strength, clutching Corner's arm, and sink my teeth into the flesh of his arm, biting down hard enough that his blood fills my mouth. He shrieks, stumbling backward, releasing me. I whirl, ready to tear his throat out with my bare hands. His back is to me as I reach for his neck, rage fueling every step—

He drops to his knees, falling face first against the ground.

An arrow is sunk straight through his eye and protruding out the back of his skull.

"What the fuck?" Erix's eyes are darting all around, looking for someone he most certainly can't see.

But I can *feel* him.

I rush toward Erix, my strength slowly returning as my primal instincts to protect my mates flood my body. In his distraction looking for Crane, I slam into him, using my entire weight to take him down.

Varian hisses as the blade drags across his throat and clatters to the ground, but it's just a scratch. I crash atop Erix and he groans, but immediately throws me off of him. My head slams against the cobblestones, knocking the breath from my lungs. I scramble backward, trying to find my feet, trying to rise as Erix bears down on me, that blade retrieved and in his hand—

Blaize darts in front of me, catching Erix with one silver hand around the throat. He groans as he lifts Erix off the ground, his eyes like ice as he glares up at him. "You should've made the poison stronger," he spits. "But your biggest mistake?" he asks while Erix's legs flail, his face turning purple as he tries to breathe. "Touching what's mine."

A loud snap cracks through the air.

Erix's eyes go dark, his head at an awkward angle.

Stars, Blaize snapped his neck. With *one* hand.

He drops him, letting all that dead, evil weight hit the ground with a thud.

"About time you showed up," Varian says, eyes cast behind me.

I'm on my feet in seconds, whirling around to see Crane. His bow in one hand, chest heaving beneath his leathers.

In that moment, I don't see my enemy.

Don't see the pain between us.

All I see is my friend, my...

I throw my arms around him. "You're here," I gasp, clinging to him. "You're really here."

He drops his bow and we sink to our knees, clinging to each other. "I never left you. I've been with you since you told me to leave. Watching. I had to wait for my shot. I couldn't risk you." He cups my cheeks in his hands. "I could never leave you, Ges," he says, then crushes his lips to mine.

I whimper against the burning kiss, all the pain seeping from the wound between us.

The wound General Payne struck.

Lightning streaks into my veins, awakening what was lost inside me, my powers bursting through the steel doors as the poison wears off. And beneath it, beneath the numbness and the buried truths, I feel Crane there as I always have.

My fourth and final mate.

He's always been there, but after what happened, I didn't want to acknowledge it.

"The general," he says, breaking our kiss. "He forced me to...I couldn't save you, Ges. He was watching me. And Erix...*stars*, Erix would've done such horrible things to you if

I tried to help. They forced me to watch and it killed me every single time. I died every time they hurt you—"

I kiss the words from his tongue, holding him tightly against me, feeling a balm over my soul at his return.

"I understand," I say. "I'm sorry I didn't listen sooner. I should've. I've been such a fool." I shake my head. "The general, his poison...I'm a fool for not seeing it. Not seeing what he was doing. Planning. I...I don't deserve to be queen."

"Don't you dare say that," Crane says, hauling us both to our feet.

"None of us saw that weapon coming," Varian says, testing his arms by shifting them back and forth. "Fucking nasty stuff."

"But that's the point," I say. "General Payne kept us chasing our tails while he developed a weapon that can render us all helpless. Do you know the advantage that gives him?"

"We know," River says, walking to me shakily. He smooths a hand over my cheek. "But this is not the end."

Tears roll down my cheeks at that declaration, and I embrace him too. Then Varian, and finally Blaize, who is still glaring down at Erix's lifeless body.

"He didn't suffer enough," Blaize says after releasing me.

I agree, but right now, I'm too broken, too filled with shame to vocalize it. "I've let you all down. Let Cari down."

"You haven't," River assures me. "You are the queen of the Shattered Isle with the support of your people. You are not alone in this."

I look to each of my mates, sucking in a sharp breath as I nod. I know I'm not alone, but I know there is so much work to be done. So much more to learn and atone for before I can proudly wear my crown again.

"We need to—"

My words are cut off by the roar of sky-ships.

We all look to the skies.

"You suppose those are the friends Payne spoke of?" Varian asks, glaring up at the half dozen ships speeding our way.

Panic slices through me as I scan the little village. Luckily, the residents have all taken cover while the general toyed with us.

"Yep," Blaize says, hands on his hips as he watches the skies.

"Probably twenty guards per ship?" River asks.

"At least," Crane says, scooping his bow off the ground.

Varian's eyes meet mine for a cruel second. "We've had worse odds, haven't we, love?"

I choke out a broken laugh because no, no we haven't.

Stars, is there no end to this?

I glance to my right, where Blaize stands, and lace my fingers through his hand. He looks down at me, not bothering to hide behind a mask. He sees the odds, sees death approaching, and doesn't cower.

"I'm with you," he says, dipping his head to brush a kiss over my lips. "Until the end."

I swallow hard, nodding as I turn to River on my left. He kisses me, silent and strong, the roar of ships drowning out any words he might've spoken as they grow closer. I move to Varian, kissing him quickly, almost harshly, as the wind from the ships whirls around us.

Last is Crane. Such devastation rings in his eyes, and I can hear the words he can't speak—*I wish we had more time.*

Me too, mates.

Me too.

We shift into a defensive line, our powers weak but

restored as the final drops of poison drain from our system, and watch as the ships land.

We can't outrun them.

They would shoot us all down in our attempt to escape.

We can only face them.

The ships' loading docks all drop, and over a hundred guards spill from the insides.

And each one has a blaster aimed right at us.

19

GESSI

Time slows down to the space between my heartbeats.

My powers are heightened to the point that I can feel insects tunneling through the dirt beneath our feet.

My instincts are keening, buzzing with electricity as I stare death in the face.

I spare one last look at my mates, turning left and right, my heart aching from the loss already. But if we're going down, at least we're going down together.

I punch the air, drawing a massive mound of dirt up with the move, trying to shield us.

Blasters crack the air, a succession of pews and pops that splinter the skies, the heat from the shots slicing right through the dirt gathering before us. We duck, flattening ourselves on the ground, trying to buy us a few more seconds.

And I look up, watching as shot after shot rings out, the guards not noticing we've dropped, not with my dirt shield still in place, and a kernel of hope blossoms in my chest. If we could just—

Everything goes dark.

Darker than midnight when the stars are covered by storm clouds.

The scent of snow and stars is everywhere, and I'm floating.

Death...Is this death?

Shadows curl around my body, lifting me and sweeping me back and back, away from the sounds of the blasters, away from the sounds of the guards—

I roll onto a patch of grass on a hilltop overlooking the main cobblestoned road below.

River lands next to me, then Blaize.

Varian and Crane are punching and kicking, clawing like cats as the shadows pull back like a thick velvet curtain.

"Are they always this dense or do I just bring it out in them?" a smooth, familiar voice asks.

I gape at the sight of Lock, one of Cari's mates, standing on the hilltop, extending his hand toward Varian.

"Shadow slinger," Varian snaps, taking his hand and hauling to his feet. "Should've known."

"You should've," Lock says, clapping him on the back. "Did you miss me, beast boy?"

"Not even a little," Varian spits.

Someone clears their throat behind me and I turn around, whimpering at the sight of Cari.

"Cari!" I can barely manage to walk a straight line to her. She rushes toward me and we clash in a tangle of arms and happy tears. "How are you here?" I ask once I pull back enough to look at her.

"Crane contacted us," she says, motioning to him behind me. "Figured you might need a visit." She glances down at the guards who are scrambling around the village looking for us. "Looks like he was right."

My heart sinks. "I've let you down," I breathe the words. "I've let everyone down. The general nearly killed us with this new power-draining poison and he's flying toward the throne as we speak."

Cari shakes her head, her long black hair pulled back in a tight braid. "You could never fail me, Gessi," she says, nothing but sincerity in her eyes. "You've been fighting for our people. Defending them no matter the cost to you. Protecting *them*, not some mound of stone and a chair my father sat on for far too long. Our people make a queendom, not some palace. The people love *you*, Gessi. They will stand with you, fight for you." She smiles at me, tears in her eyes as she presses her forehead against mine.

I close my eyes, leaning into her embrace. "I want to make you proud."

"You've made me proud every day since we were younglings sneaking out of the palace with the sole intent of irritating the hell out of Varian and Crane," she says.

"You two *were* irritating as all shit," Varian says from behind me. "Used to sneak barnacles into my bed. Prickly little fuckers."

We both laugh, the sensation filling my lungs with air.

Cari releases me, stepping back to her mate's side.

Blaize and River are nodding thanks to Lock, who accepts it with a relaxed smile. Varian and Crane hug Cari, and for a few blissful heartbeats, there is nothing but this much-needed reunion.

Commotion rises from the village below us, the guards now cracking shots at something moving too fast for my eyes to follow at first. The bright blaster shots are bouncing off of something...a shield?

"Fucking hell, Lock," Blaize growls as he races to the tip of the hill. "You could've told me you brought Steel."

"I was going to mention it," Lock says, glancing down at his brother now single-handily taking on an army of a hundred of the general's guards.

"Get me down there. Now." There is no room for question in Blaize's tone.

Lock glances around at each of us, rubbing his hands together. "Now that we're all better prepared," he says, grinning deviously. "Should we go dispatch them?"

One nod from all of us and his shadows swirl, transporting us down to the village, down to the fight.

The second they peel back enough for me to see, I watch as a spiderweb of sharp shadow flings out from the epicenter of our group, laying waste to half the guards in one blow.

Shock ripples through me at the display of power, but Cari merely rolls her eyes and says, "Show off."

Lock grins at her. "You know you love it when I play with my shadows," he teases in an intimate voice that doesn't at all fit with the battle we're currently in.

Cari winks at him, winding her fingers through the air, sending ice daggers and spears through any guard that looks our way.

My mates join the fray, and I shift into fight mode. Drawing on power fueled by the four mating bonds inside me and the sister bond beside me. There will be no loss on our side now, not with the strength of Cari and her mates and mine combined.

Together we are unstoppable.

Together we will not be broken.

Branches and vines snap anywhere I walk, slicing and cutting through the guards trying to turn my mates and friends to dust. A whirl of blood and fighting surrounds us, wearing us down to the mere dregs of our power as we push back against them.

    Until my fingers are sore from wielding my powers.

    Until I can barely breathe from running and fighting.

    Until there is nothing left of the unit but bodies.

    Until we stand united in exhaustion, but victory.

GESSI

"We haven't seen any sign of him yet, your majesty," Lance says through the drone connection Steel sent his way hours ago. "But I assure you, my assassins are ready and alert. He won't break our borders."

I breathe out a sigh of relief. "Thank you, Lance. We will make our way back to you as soon as we can."

"We'll be waiting," he says. "Stay safe, your majesty."

I nod to him, then click off the drone, which curls in on itself and flies back over to Steel, who is lounging on a couch across the room, Cari in the middle, and Lock on the other side.

The village was kind enough to give us several large rooms for the night after we helped them clean up what wreckage we could and assured them they were safe for now.

It's only a matter of time before the general realizes the ships he sent aren't carting me back to the palace, but he hasn't attacked or made a play for the throne yet.

Why? That question will nag me until I know his next move.

I make my way across the room, joining Crane on another couch across from Cari. Blaize and River and Varian sit at an oak table a few feet away, finishing up the meal provided to us earlier.

"Lance says there have been no signs of General Payne," I say, leaning back on the couch, my arm brushing Crane's. Sparks of need flash through me at the innocent touch, and my eyes meet his for a brief moment.

We haven't fully spoken or been alone since he returned. I know it needs to happen, but this conversation is more important right now. As is always the case with Crane and me.

Cari tilts her head. "And he said he was leaving to take the throne when he left you all with Erix and Corner?"

I nod, the weight of what happened...what *almost* happened...threatening to crush my chest. "He said he was sending Erix's friends to pick him up, me as their prisoner as leverage against you, and to kill my mates," I choke on the last part, then breathe past it. "Then he said he had a throne to claim."

"Perhaps he's studying your new guards," Cari says. "Maybe the forces protecting the throne are stronger than he anticipated."

"If that's the case," I say. "Then we can hopefully intercept him before he has a chance to attempt an attack."

Lock slides his arm around Cari. "And the poison," Lock says, his midnight hair hanging down to his shoulders. "You said it only lasted a little while?"

I nod again, cringing at the memory. "Ten minutes, maybe fifteen."

Steel shifts on the couch, leaning his elbows on his

knees, his palms together. "That's enough time. Ten minutes without our powers is like an eternity, as I'm sure you felt, Gessi."

"A nightmare," Varian says as he rises from the table, stopping to lean against a wooden pillar near the couch where I sit. His shift ripples beneath his skin, as if he needs reassurance it's still there. "I've never felt anything like it—"

"I have," I say, shaking my head. Crane slides his fingers into mine, a new sort of pain settling between us.

General Payne forced Crane to watch. Took his innate abilities at seeing across distances vast and wide, took his pleasure of watching from a hidden, peaceful spot, and turned it against him. He suffered more than me, I realize with terrible clarity. Because I would not be able to watch as my mates suffered, not that I'm sure Crane even realizes we're mates, but still. It would ruin me.

"The chains," Crane says, his voice like broken glass.

Cari's hands curl into fists, the temperature in the room dropping a few degrees.

"I'm fine," I assure the room, since mostly everyone is either wearing looks of pity or concern, neither of which I need.

Except for Blaize. Stars, I love that male. He never looks at me with anything other than a challenge or unbridled need.

"We need to move on the palace." I sit straighter, eyes on Cari. "I'm not asking you to be away from the All Plane more than you already are. We can do this alone."

Cari waves me off. "Talon and Tor have the All Plane under control. With Storm's new position as the king's advisor, I'm sure him and Talon are outfitting the palace with all kinds of unbelievable tech," she says, a soft smile on her lips. It's quickly replaced by the seriousness of our current situation. "I know you don't need my help, Ges," she continues, and I furrow my brow at her. "But I'm here. We're here." She motions to her mates. "And we will stand with you."

My heart expands in my chest and I nod my gratitude to each of them before blowing out a breath. "All right," I say with more conviction. "We will set off for the Shattered Isle royal city tomorrow. Enough time for us to restore our powers fully and contemplate figuring out an antidote to General Payne's new weapon." I shake my head. "All that time I spent in the dungeon and I never once thought to study the chains. Honestly, I tried to stay as far away from them as possible whenever I wasn't in them. And now he's weaponized it." I bite my bottom lip, chewing over the possibilities.

"You couldn't have been expected to do that," River says from where he sits before his empty plate at the table. "Not under the circumstances."

"I know," I say. "Just wish I had. We'd have a better idea of how to counteract the effects."

"So we go into the dungeons," Blaize says, arms folded over his chest as he leans back in his chair at the table, his legs stretched out. "We get those chains and figure it out."

"That's a start," I say, feeling slightly better from the plan already. "But we still don't know what exactly he's used to concoct it."

"Then we catch him and torture him until he tells us." Varian grins, his partially shifted teeth adding to the venom in his eyes. "Who's with me?"

River raises his hand, then Blaize and Crane. Steel does the same a few moments later.

Lock's eyes dart between them and he shakes his head. "I'm not really a team player kind of male," he says, and Cari laughs, nudging him in the ribs. "But I'm all for torture," he amends, bowing toward me as he says it.

And I can't help it, a chuckle slips from my lips.

The tension in the room breaks with the new plan of action and we fall into a silence as we sip on drinks.

"Maybe he knows we took out six of his ships today," Cari says. "Maybe that's what is making him pause."

"I doubt those six ships were the only ones he had in his arsenal. Not with the way he's been attacking villages and cities across the Isle. He's been doing more than making poison."

"Likely gathering followers and supplies for the war," Lock says matter of factly. He raises his brows when Cari and I look at him with shocked faces. "What?" he asks. "It's what I would be doing if I wanted to steal a throne. I'd make certain I had a formidable yet disposable army with enough weapons to make the battle barely even a fight."

"Oh, stars," I say, rubbing my temples. "Of course, that's what he's doing. I never thought he was merely hiding and attacking out of spite, but I honestly didn't think anyone would follow him, except for those who were already under his boot."

"Maybe no one has," Cari says hopefully. "He's vile to deal with on his best days and he hasn't been having many of those since I killed my father."

The reality of too many *what-ifs* in this equation pile up behind my eyes in the form of one hell of a headache.

"We will get him," Cari assures me. "Right now, you need to focus on healing. Recharging. We're going to need every ounce of strength to finish this."

I nod, knowing she's right. We have a plan, all we can do now is heal and follow it. I just hate that sense of dread lingering in the pit of my stomach, the one that whispers cold bits of doubt in my ear, things like I'll never be able to catch him, the ruthless general who has decades upon decades of experience over me.

Eventually, the conversation turns to more peaceful, less stressful topics, like Cari's new role as All Plane queen and how she's adjusted to living under the sun. And after a couple hours, Steel and Lock whisk Cari away to their room, nothing but fire in their eyes as they each touch the other, all connected in one beautiful display of love.

And for a few moments, I allow myself to bask in that, in the fact that Cari is here, safe and healthy and whole, and that I too have survived and my mates along with me.

Crane stands up after they've left, approaching Blaize, Varian, and River. "Can I beg a favor?" he asks, and Varian is the first to cock a brow at him.

"What is it?" Varian asks.

"Can I please have some time alone with Ges?" Crane asks, and my lips part.

Blaize steps into his space, brow furrowed. "We almost died today," he says, his voice icy. "No way in hell you're keeping our mate to yourself all night."

Lava slides beneath my skin at the primal dominance in Blaize's tone, at the way River and Varian are nodding their agreement. I can't blame them, my entire being is reaching out for all of them right now, fueled by almost losing them earlier. But Crane...we do have unfinished business to discuss.

"Have you lot forgotten that I'm capable of making my own decisions?" I ask, crossing the room to stand between them, who are all now on their feet, staring each other down like another brawl is about to break out.

"My queen," River says. "You know all you have to do is ask and we'll leave," he continues, slipping his hand into mine and drawing it to his lips. He presses a searing kiss to the back of my hand before releasing it.

Warm shivers race across my skin from the gesture, from his words. "I know," I say, smiling at each of them. "An hour," I say. "Then join us." I glance nervously at Crane. "You can decide then if you want to stay or not."

Crane dips his head.

Varian points a finger at him. "One hour. No more, no less."

Blaize merely glares at him before following Varian out of the room.

River, the last to leave, claps Crane on his shoulder and says, "Good luck," before joining Varian and Blaize outside.

And then it's just Crane and me and the vast expanse of the room. The wood floors flicker under the candles melting down on various tables, the white wax pooling like beads of frozen water at the base. There are couches and a hutch with food and drinks, and connected in the farthest corner is a door that leads to a bedroom.

My nerves tangle the longer I stand there cataloguing the room instead of thinking of something to say to the male who has broken my heart and put it back together so many times I've lost count.

"You wanted me alone," I finally say. "And yet you stand there, silent and watchful as usual?"

Crane releases a rough breath, eyes finding the floor. "I've rehearsed this a thousand times in my head but now that the moment is here, my words are tangled."

I swallow around the lump in my throat, crossing the distance to stand right in front of him. Timidly, I reach out and smooth my hand over his cheek, sighing when he allows the touch, when he doesn't fly away from the connection.

"I know what the general made you do," I say. "He told me. I...I didn't know," I say. "I thought...I thought..."

Crane's eyes darken. "You thought I would willingly stand there and watch you get hurt."

Shame slides over my skin and I drop my hand, curling in on myself. "What would you have thought? You are my oldest friend, the one who taught me how to shoot a bow on the beach under the stars."

"I'm more than your oldest friend," he says, and my heart races in my chest. "You know that now, don't you?"

I tip my chin, meeting his eyes. "What am I supposed to know, Crane?" I ask, sighing. "That you've spent the days since my torture arguing with me at every turn? Always siding against my ideas, my plans. That you seem more at ease when you are away from me rather than at my side? You may not have stood idly by and watched as the general and Erix tortured me, and I'm sorry for what they made you do to keep me safe from something worse, but you never once agreed with me—"

"I argued for your sake!" he snaps, the words ricocheting in the room. He steps closer, our bodies flush as he gently grips the back of my neck. "The thought of you being harmed again," he says, softer this time, his eyes flickering over my face. "I couldn't stand it, Ges. Couldn't bare it if something happened to you again and I wasn't there to stop it. I couldn't be helpless again, powerless to prevent the pain, to stop the suffering. And you chasing after the general led to exactly that."

My palms flatten on his broad chest, an ache wrenching between my thighs at how close we stand, at that glistening string of light stretching taut between us. "I am the queen of the Shattered Isle, Crane," I say, breathless. "It's me and me alone who has to take responsibility for the actions of

General Payne and you know it. I can't send innocent assassins out to stop him, not when I know first-hand how brutal he is. It's *me*. I have to end this."

"I know," he breathes, eyes darting from my lips to my eyes. "I know that now. I knew it while I watched you, followed you as you fought to protect the people, the places you visited. I know I was wrong, Ges. Just after failing you once, I didn't...*couldn't* fail you again."

"You didn't," I say. "You saved me. From what Erix would've done...and today, you saved me again. Crane, you..." I can't find the right things to say. There are too many scars between us that are hard to climb over. "I've always loved you," I say. "Even before I knew you were my...mate."

His eyes widen at the word, and something clangs down our bond like lightning.

"You know it," he says. "You finally feel it."

"How long have you known?" I ask.

"Long enough to know you deserve better than me."

I shake my head. "That's not your decision to make."

He nods, his lips drawing closer. "I know," he says. "I'm done trying to protect you from me. You don't need me to. You're perfectly capable of protecting yourself. But, if you'll let me, I will spend the rest of my forever making it up to you."

"Yes," I say on a breath, tipping my head back even more. "Yes, please."

Crane's lips crash against mine, a carnal kiss that has me clinging to him like a wild, desperate creature. His tongue slides over mine, hungry and exploring. Tasting. Savoring. Stars, his mouth. It's wild and sharp, warm and consuming.

I arch against him, needing to be closer, needing to feel him—

Crane breaks our kiss, stepping *away* from me. His eyes

are molten as he looks me up and down, then shakes his head. "I haven't earned you yet," he says, and I arch a brow at him. He motions to the couch behind me. "But I want to watch you touch yourself."

Heat soars inside me at his words. "Crane," I say, a question and plea. But he simply shakes his head again, backing up to the opposite couch, settling into it and stretching his arms along the back, like he needs something to hold onto.

"This is my punishment," he says. "I can't have you. Not until I earn you."

"But the bond," I say, almost begging.

"Will be there forever," he says. "As long as you don't reject it."

"Never," I say.

A smile turns up the corners of his lips. "Then what are you waiting for?"

A challenge and a need.

I slide out of the simple cotton pants and shirt I'd changed into after battle, and let them drop to the floor.

Crane's jaw tightens as his eyes roam over my body, lingering on my scars. He shifts on the couch as if he might get up and touch me, but he holds himself there by some scrap of will I don't possess. I want nothing more than to cross the distance and perch on his lap, but if this is the game he wants to play, I'm more than in. Besides, I've always known how much he likes to watch.

"Clock is ticking," he finally says, and I smirk at him.

"Are you worried?" I ask, slowly sitting on the opposite couch. "About what will happen when my mates come in here?"

Something dark and dangerous flashes over his eyes, making all sorts of tingles erupt over my body.

"I'm not worried, Ges. I'm ready. To accept this role in

your life, to be there for you and for them. We're in this together. As long as you'll have me."

"I will," I say.

"Then prove it," he teases.

I lay back on the couch, my fingers trembling as I glide them delicately over my skin. Down my neck, over my breasts, down the curves of my stomach, and finally between my thighs.

Leather creaks as I dip my fingers into my aching heat, and I turn my head to see Crane gripping the back of the couch so hard he looks like he'll tear right through it. I smile at him, slow and languid, my eyes glazed with need as I continue my own exploration.

"Fuck, Ges," he groans as I circle my clit with one hand and tease my nipple with the other. "You're so fucking beautiful."

"You sure you don't want to join me?" I ask, sliding my fingers through my wetness, slipping inside and gasping as I do it over and over again. My eyes on his and his on mine, the sensation like nothing else with him watching me do something that normally I'd do alone.

"More than anything," he growls. "But only when I've earned it."

"Who determines that?" I ask, breathless.

"Me," he says, his voice tight. "Arch your hips," he demands, and warmth floods my veins at the command.

I arch my hips, rocking upward, my fingers dipping deeper, driving me to that edge I can feel riding up to my body.

"Crane," I sigh his name, increasing my pace, losing myself in this moment with him.

"Stars," he groans. "Look at you," he says. "I love the way

you chase your pleasure. You're so close, baby. Are you going to make yourself come for me?"

His words are like licks of flame across my skin, the bond between us rippling with need as I rock against myself.

"Yes," I breathe the word, arching higher, sinking deeper into myself as I plunge over that edge. "Yes," I moan, my orgasm vibrating over my skin, sending delightful shivers all along my bones as I come down.

When I open my eyes, Crane is there, hovering over me but not touching. "Beautiful," he whispers, then flicks his eyes downward where my hand is resting on my stomach. He kneels, lowering his lips to my hand, and sucks my fingers into his mouth, moaning around them. I gasp at the sensation, then whimper when he pulls back. "Delicious tease," he says, holding my gaze.

"Now this looks promising," Varian says as he saunters into the room, River and Blaize behind him. Blaize locks the door before he comes to stand near us.

Crane smirks at him, then winks at me before backing up to the couch on the opposite side again.

"I didn't mean you had to leave," Varian teases him, already yanking his shirt over his head. River and Blaize doing the same. "But like we said before, we almost died today. Claiming our mate *will* happen."

My toes curl against the leather as I watch them undress, watch the three of them look at me like I'm their salvation.

"Understood," Crane says, settling back into the couch. "I'm content to watch. For now."

Varian cocks a brow at him, looking between him and me and back again. "Oh, it's about damn time, friend," he says, smiling at Crane.

"He's the last, right?" River asks me, and I laugh.

"The last," I say.

"Good," River says. "I'm not against sharing, but it's getting really crowded."

"We'll take turns," Varian says, winking at River.

And while everyone else is talking, Blaize is ignoring them, eyes only for me as he leans over the couch, sliding those silver fingers around my throat where I still lay on the couch. My body comes alive with sensation, awakening at that dominate, primal touch.

He tugs, lifting me effortlessly, bringing my mouth to his. I gasp between his lips, feeling the pressure at my throat as he uses his other hand to haul me onto the back of the couch, legs spread for him to step between.

Blaize glides his hard cock through my wetness, teasing me, holding me with one arm behind my lower back, the other on my throat.

"Just because there are four of us," he says, low and gravelly. "Doesn't mean I'm always going to share you." The promise in his words has me turning liquid. "Now, tell me, who do you belong to?" He increases the pressure at my throat at the same time he slides his cock inside me an inch, making my eyes roll back with pleasure. "Say it," he demands, pulling out all the way.

"You," I gasp. "*You.*"

"Good girl." Blaize plunges inside me, seating himself to the hilt before pulling out and doing it all over again. I grip the back of the couch where I'm perched, holding on as he fucks me like we're the only two people in the room.

"Fuck," Crane says from behind me, and I spare a glance over my shoulder. He's watching us with that predator's gaze of his, still clinging to the couch instead of touching himself. His rules, his punishment. One even I don't think he deserves.

River and Varian break out of a kiss, both heading in

opposite directions. River comes around the couch, almost timidly as he approaches my side, kissing my shoulder, my arm, his hands roaming over the spaces of my body untouched by Blaize.

Varian steps onto the couch behind me, kneeling just enough to line himself up with my ass. And in some unspoken line of connection, Blaize shifts me just enough to give him access and then I'm gasping as Varian's shifted fingers tease my tight hole while he nips at my neck.

"Blaize," Varian says, and Blaize's eyes snap to Varian behind me. "Let me get a little," he says, not asks, and Blaize glares at him before slowing his pace inside me. Varian smirks as Blaize pulls out, and I'm immediately filled with Varian's fingers as he pumps me a few times, making my thighs clench around Blaize's waist before he drags those fingers beneath me, swirling the wetness around and inside that sensitive, tight space.

I moan, my body crackling with electricity as they wind me up into a tight rope of need. River captures the moan with his mouth at the same time Blaize slides home again, pounding into me with the need of a mate who almost lost today.

We all almost lost each other today and my heart...my heart would not survive such a thing.

"Never again," I say against River's mouth, drawing back enough to cup his cheek. I whimper as Varian slides into me from behind, him and Blaize filling me so much I'm consumed by the two.

River shakes his head, kissing me again, his tongue sliding over mine as Varian and Blaize find a rhythm as my entire body tightens around them.

"Never again," Blaize growls, each of them fully understanding the promise we're making.

"Not a chance, love," Varian says. "This sweet ass is mine forever." He lightly smacks my ass right as he pumps into me, the pain edged in pleasure, causing me to flutter around Blaize's cock.

"Fuck," Blaize growls. "Harder," he demands, upping his pace.

The sounds of our bodies clashing together only fuel the desire crashing down our bonds, all these beautiful chains of light with a signature to the owner rippling and stretching and aching.

Varian smacks my ass again, plunging deeper, the two moving in sync. I throw my head back, resting it against Varian's broad chest, and River leaps on the opportunity to worship my breasts.

Stars.

I can't.

These males.

My mates.

My assassins.

They are my salvation and my undoing.

My pain and my pleasure.

My passion and my calm.

"Mate!" I cry out as my body builds and twists and twines toward a crescendo I'm helpless against. "Mate," I say again, unable to single out one of them. Not when each of them is working me into a frenzy, sending me into an orbit where nothing exists but this. This love between us, this carnal need, this endless well of bliss.

"One more time, Varian," Blaize demands.

Varian slides out, spanking me one more time as he and Blaize both pump into me at the same time—

I explode.

Combust.

My entire body is a river of pleasure and electricity as it cascades down my body, from the crown of my head to the tip of my toes. The release keeps coming, crashing inside me like ocean waves, relentless and consuming. I can barely catch my breath from the force of it and yet I'm content to float in its current forever.

"Gessi," Blaize groans as he spills inside me.

"Love," Varian says at the same time.

River slows his kisses, his own release warm as it slides down my thigh from where he'd been stroking himself.

"Promise me," I finally say once we've all come down but are still connected. "Promise me we'll never let that happen again."

Blaize's eyes are on mine as he nods. Varian kisses my shoulder in response, River doing the same to my neck.

None of them are vocalizing the promise, because they all know we can't control what happens next. But with the four of them? I feel like I *can* control the stars and moon and everything beyond.

For them, my mates, I can do anything.

And I will do anything to ensure we're never as close to being cleaved apart as we were today.

Crane's footsteps are silent in the room, but I feel him come around the couch before I finally see him. "Give her to me now," he says, his voice strained as he outstretches his arms. "Let me take care of her."

Blaize and Varian gently shift out of me, and I'm moved from one pair of arms to the next. Crane carefully, gently carries me to the attached bedroom and cleans me up with such tenderness that it brings tears to my eyes. He makes me drink three whole glasses of water in between a bedtime snack, all the while telling me stories from our past, making me smile in the midst of exhaustion.

The sounds of laughter from the other room are a comfort as my mates eat and drink and replenish themselves before likely taking up the spaces on the couches to sleep.

When I've done all that Crane's demanded to help care for myself, he wraps me in the blanket on the bed and settles himself behind me, content to hold me through the night.

And for this blissful moment, it feels like a space in time that even war can't touch.

21

GESSI

"G es," Cari's voice cracks, almost as if she's crying as she calls to me from outside my door.

I'm dressed and rushing to open it in a matter of seconds, my mates already waiting for me. The sun is still up, so I know we haven't slept long.

Cari's eyes are devastated and rimmed in rage as she stomps into the room, Lock and Steel following behind her with similar looks. Steel carries an ebony box and sits it on the table where we ate just hours ago.

Dread spreads like ice in my stomach.

"What's happened?" I ask, trying my best to reorient myself into my body. The sleep I'd been in was deep and peaceful and downright bliss-fueled after what happened between me and my mates last night...all of them.

"The general," Cari says, and she doesn't need to say more. Not with the way she's looking at the box. "This arrived this morning. Brone, the Jasmine Falls leader, didn't open it, brought it straight to me."

I eye the box, unable to ignore how the bottom is wet, like it's soaked in...

I stomp across the room, fingers jerking beneath the wooden lid and ripping it off—

I stumble backward, into the awaiting arms of River. I turn to face him, tears spilling down my cheeks. "No," I say, my entire body shaking. "No, no, *no.*"

Blaize and Varian and Crane take their turns looking into the box, hissing and cursing as Blaize puts the lid back on it.

I close my eyes, burying my head into River's chest, but I can't *unsee* what I just saw.

Lance.

His usual warm blue eyes, his always pristine blond hair...lifeless and covered in blood, his mouth twisted in a silent, agonized scream.

My responsibility. He was my responsibility. And he's dead. Gone. The general...how much of my people's blood did he spill?

"Gessi," Cari says, her voice full of compassion and strength I can't seem to find.

River shifts until I'm passed from him to Cari, her bracing my shoulders as she forces me to look her in the eyes.

And once I do, once I lock onto her, I find myself again. I kick up through the rough waters of panic and grief and break the surface. I breathe in deeply, finding nothing but rage boiling my blood, evaporating all the tears. It's only through the angered clarity that I see the room, see the spindly vines stretching along the walls, slithering and tightening around every available surface like snakes. And they're all dusted with snow, Cari's own response to the assault that's been delivered.

"There was a note," Cari says once we both are breathing evenly.

"What did it say?" I manage to ask, still clinging to Cari.

Lock steps around us, focusing on me. "That if you try to take back the throne, it will be the innocents in the royal city whose heads fill these boxes. Be grateful it was just him and his pathetic band of assassins that fell."

I cringe against the general's words.

My fault. I should've been stronger. Should've stopped him—

"This blood is not on your hands," Lock says, as if he read my mind. From the way he's looking at me, he did. "Put this blame where it belongs."

I let those words sink into me, accept them, and cling to them like a lifeline.

Before I can open my mouth to declare an all-out war against the general, to say we will do no such thing he asks, a resident from the village sprints into the room, doubling over from the run.

"What is it now?" Blaize asks, wary.

"Messages," the resident says. "They're burning."

"Who is?" I demand.

"Many," he breathes. "The orchard village, the herbalists, and more. We're receiving distress calls from all over the Isle, your majesty."

The vines in the room start snapping in my rage, gouging marks into the wood in their fury. Ice spiderwebs its way over them, the sharp slivers mirrors to my vines.

I look to Cari, my mirror in so many ways, and we nod at the same time.

"Tell them we're coming," I say and the words send the rest of the room into action. Steel announces he'll prepare their ship while my mates and Lock follow, grabbing their weapons as they go.

Cari and I remain.

I reach for her hand, squeezing it in promise.

"This will end," Cari says, gripping my hand.

"And there will be a reckoning," I say, and the words brand my soul with a death promise.

THE END

22

LOCK

"How many did you bring in today?" Huxton, the leader of the Onyx City, asks as he offers me a large goblet of wine. He slides the golden cup across the smooth ebony table in one of his many council rooms.

I lean up from my chair, exhaustion clinging to my bones as I reach for the offering and take a large gulp. The sparkling liquid does little to reinvigorate my powers, but they're on their last dregs.

"Two-hundred and sixty-three," I say, and Huxton's golden eyes widen.

"Stars," he says, shaking his head. "Have you slept?"

I pause with the goblet poised at my lips, my eyes on the swirling liquid inside as I shake my head. "*She* hasn't," I say, taking another generous gulp.

My mate.

My beautiful, ruthless mate.

She nor Gessi have slept since that forsaken box was sent to our chambers in Jasmine Falls.

Four nights. Four days. It's been a never-ending cycle

where our efforts were split. Steel and I flying to one village or city in need, Gessi and Cari to another, her mates to another, saving as many as we can.

"You need rest," Huxton says, leaning back in his chair.

Thank the stars for him, for his formidable city. We wouldn't have had anywhere to take those we saved if it weren't for him.

"I will," I say, setting down the now empty glass. "When she does." I tap the glass, pushing back from the table. "Thank you for that," I say, standing before him. "For all of it." Normally I'm not one for bouts of vocalized gratitude, but he's earned it. A true ally, one even the All Plane will never forget.

"Like I told your queen and mine," he says, rising to walk with me out of the room. "We are with them."

The shadows in my blood flicker with starvation, as if they've been deprived the basic needs of water and food and oxygen. I'm drained, so very drained, but with my abilities of transporting people through the shadows, I was the only one capable of saving so many.

And I wouldn't damn these people because I needed a fucking nap.

"Are there any more?" Huxton asks as we stop outside the room he's given me and Cari and Steel.

Talon and Tor will eventually make the trip, once they ready the All Plane soldiers we can spare.

"No," I say. "I think that's the last of them." I rest my hand on the knob, feeling almost too weak to turn it, to remain standing, but I don't dare let it show.

Thirteen-thousand. We saved about thirteen-thousand among the tens of thousands who suffered the recent attacks wrought by the general. He bided his time. Waited until he had the throne, to show his hand.

His army is formidable and the sky-ships and weapons he's gathered are even more so...we still haven't figured out who is supplying him.

"Good," Huxton says, knowing better than to reach out to me, to do something as foolish as grip my shoulder in support. He's smarter than that, but I see it in his eyes, feel it along the edges of his mind that I'm too tired to protect against. "My people will care for them, find places for all of them," he says. "You need to rest. Your queen does too. They all do."

I nod, feeling as if he breathed too hard I would fall over.

I've never pushed myself this hard for this long.

Huxton gives me another nod, then heads down the hallway, his long gait eating up the space in ample time, leaving me alone outside my door.

Finally, I turn the knob, my vision blurring around the edges as I close the door behind me.

"Cari," I say when I see her through the fog in my eyes. She's gorgeous, brutally exhausted, the skin beneath her eyes a deep indigo rather than the glittering blue I'm used to.

She's doctoring a wound on her arm, a cut just beneath her night-blooming-flower tattoo, the thin black lines of ink now stained with blood.

I furrow my brow, instinct roaring, blaring to go to her, but I can't move.

I can't make my feet move.

"Cari," I say again, the world tilting on its axis.

I drop to my knees, the breath rushing from my lungs.

"Lock!"

Cari calls my name.

I hear her rushed footsteps toward me, but I can't see her anymore.

There is nothing but darkness.

My shadows curl inside me, *around* me, and jerk me backward down a long tunnel with no end in sight.

THE END

THANK you so much for reading! The next book in the series, THE RECKONING, will release early 2023! If you haven't read the first two books in the series featuring Cari and her mates be sure to check out HER VILLAINS and HER REVENGE in Kindle Unlimited!

LET'S CHAT

I love hearing from you! You can find me at the following places!

TikTok @JadePresleyAuthor
  Instagram
  Facebook
  Facebook Author Page
  Jadempresley@gmail.com
  LinkTree
  BookBub
  And be sure to sign up for my newsletter here for release information, cover reveals, and giveaways!

ACKNOWLEDGMENTS

A GIANT thank you must be paid to all the amazing, badass booktokers out there that have been so amazing and supportive! The list below is just a snapshot of the wonderful readers out there and if I missed your name, PLEASE know that I see you and appreciate every mention, video, comment, and message! I love you all!

@tiffandbooks @daniisbookish @winterarrow @trishaarwood @pixiepages @oliveroseandco @thebookishgirlreviews @asthebookends @breanna_reads @booksdanirreads @songreads @erynsarchive @yelenabooks @hdouglas92 @leggothemeggoreads @klaudias_bookdiary @libraryofmadison @stakestheworld @thebookcloud @spicybooks @sami_cantstopreading @rachies_book_nook @dealingdreams @booklovingcorgimom @coffeeandbookswithlauran @lokiquinn1993 @nightowlbooks @bookofcons @animebaby33 @muddy_orbs @crysreads @biblio_mama @briannareadds @morallygrayreads @fortheloveofbooksandwine @natashareadsnrambles @pagel_bagel_ @nerdy_julith @bookishmot @jvstjewels @breereadsromance_ @moonnoodledesigns @thebookishlifeofchels @touch.my.shelf @once.upon.a.bookshelf @dani.reads.books @dumbSong @ireadromancetoescape @spidersamii @jazzyjay121 @sixhorizonreads @da_vincis_daughter @mary_a_light_official @beautyandthebookcase @rachelptrsm12 @the_bookishsiren @nicolasbooks @thatreadingmom @feral.for.fiction @katiemurphy18

@readswithcoffee @the8thhorcurx @chelsbellsbooklover @candicereads   @mjmona89   @raquel.reads   @meg-gintheempath   @bookishvader   @thiscrazybookishlife @hreads2much @ashtonthescorpio @e_paletta @nofergirl @jaclynoiler @laney1811 @booktok.books1011 @helenwyn43 @sassyboots4

Another huge thanks to Amber Hodge for editing this and making it sparkle! I couldn't do this series without you!

A big thanks to my husband and family who always indulge me when I get lost in the writing cave.

And finally, a huge shout out to all the Marvel fans who just want a little more sometimes :)

ABOUT THE AUTHOR

Jade Presley is a pen name for a fantasy and contemporary romance author who loves cranking out stories about seriously sexy males and the sassy women who bring them to their knees. She's a wife, mother, and board game connoisseur.

Printed in Great Britain
by Amazon

16403733R00132